A Verbania Novel

COTTON CANDY NOTES

Lovey LaRue

By Lovey LaRue

<u>Standalones</u>
Part-Time Husband

<u>A Verbania Novel</u>
Cotton Candy Notes

To my husband. Always.

***

Content Warnings

FMC= Female Main Character/MMC= Male Main Character

Gaslighting/mental abuse from partner (not between FMC and MMC)

Stalking by partner (not between FMC and MMC)

Open Marriage (not between FMC and MMC)

Emotional betrayal within marriage (not between FMC and MMC)

Feels like cheating (not between FMC and MMC)

Dating to make partner jealous (not between FMC and MMC)

Violence (fist fighting, no weapons)

Weight shaming by partner (not between FMC and MMC)

Body shaming (one chapter not ongoing)

Falling in love while legally married

Mild drug use (cannabis)

Graphic sexual content

Profanity

"WE'RE MARRIED, BETHY! CAN you believe it?" Trevor asks, hugging me.

We're in the back of the limo on the way to our reception. My princess gown is poofing around us, my cheeks are aching from smiling. Trevor is so handsome in his dark suit and ruby-red tie. I can't believe we're finally married. I lean over to kiss him, but he touches my face and pulls back a smidge. "I don't want to smudge your lipstick."

I want to tell him it doesn't matter, but we arrive at our super snazzy venue. Trevor was really involved with the wedding planning—this location was his choice. He made a lot of the decisions, actually. His mother insisted that we have an elegant wedding so we wouldn't embarrass her. I wanted something fun, colorful, and maybe a little kitschy, but I was vetoed. No matter—the wedding was beautiful.

And marriage isn't about the wedding, anyway, but about the love between Trevor and me.

We get out of the car and walk into the waiting arms of our family and friends. Hugs and congratulations escort us into the lovely reception hall. Somewhere along the way, I lost my new husband but found my parents and brother.

"Pretty damn fancy, Pigeon," my brother Danny says, using his pet name for me. I'm a plump woman, and my family swears I look like a pigeon with a cinched waist. I love it. Too bad pigeons don't have cherry-red hair and a flair for vintage styles—then he'd be totally right.

"Yeah, you can definitely tell the twerp had a hand in the planning," my dad complains.

"Oh, Daddy, I love how everything turned out!" I say, brightly, stifling the part of me that's disappointed.

"You love white tablecloths, gold chandeliers, and red roses?" Danny harumphs.

No. But I love Trevor.

"Your dream wedding involved pink, blue, and an Elvis impersonator. No way in hell this was your choice." My mom raises her eyebrows.

"That was ages ago. I've grown up since then," I say, laughing, ignoring the ache in my chest screaming that this wedding was a mistake.

Danny rolls his eyes. "It was a year ago."

"Shut up." I nudge him in the side.

"I guess I should start calling you all mom and dad, huh?" Trevor pushes his way into our small group. He grabs my hand and tugs me to him, kissing my temple.

My parents laugh stiffly, but Danny rolls his eyes, earning himself another jab in the side.

"Come on, Bethy. My grandparents' lawyer wants to meet you. You can see your parents any time."

I glance at my family apologetically and let Trevor lead me away. Danny scoffs, and my parents have matching expressions of exasperation. He doesn't mean to be so abrupt. He's excited to show me off.

We find his mom hanging on the arm of a handsome older man, simpering up at him. She was beautiful once—perhaps she still is—but I can't see it beyond her bitterness that Trevor picked me.

"Trevor! What took you so long?" She pulls him away from me, threading her arm into his.

"We were talking to Bethany's family," he says, rolling his eyes.

"Well, young lady, I've looked over your prenup, and it looks good. Got to protect our Trevor, just in case anything happens. You're going to be a homemaker, aren't you?" the older man says, winking at me.

"Well, actually, I'm going to—"

"Of course she is!" Trevor interrupts me with a sharp glance.

We've discussed it, of course, and Trevor really wants me to stay home. But I want a career, something to do with books. I've always dreamed of opening a little bookshop.

Trevor thinks that idea is silly—why would I want to stress myself out when I don't have to?

I know Trevor is getting irritated, so I smile and agree. Not like I'm actually going to be a stay-at-home wife. That would be ridiculous.

The next hour is a whirlwind of cheek kisses and unfamiliar faces. Most of the guests are strangers to me. I never considered how large the guest list would end up. I have a small family. My parents are only children of only children, so it has always been just us.

The wedding planner—handpicked by Trevor's mom—is hustling us to the beautiful white three-tier cake surrounded by red roses. Trevor is grinning and tugging me along. His happiness settles my soul, making this whole affair worth it.

"Don't smash that cake in my face," I whisper to him as the DJ announces it's time to cut the cake.

He smirks at me.

Damn it.

We cut our slices and face each other.

"Please don't get cake on my face," I whisper again.

"Oh, Bethy, don't be so serious," he replies, sticking his finger in the icing and tapping my nose. My eyes tingle, but I laugh to keep the tears at bay, and we feed each other a bite of cake.

Trevor looks down at me and kisses my nose, licking the icing off his lips, then kisses my forehead.

I'm going to love this man forever, I remind myself.

One

Betty

I LOVE MY HUSBAND.

I love my husband.

I love my husband.

But why can't he pick up his own underwear?

Why in the hell am I the one picking it up?

I sigh, knowing the answer. Because he won't. If I want to live in a clean house, I have to clean it. The bastard would live in filth without me.

Today is our fifth anniversary. I asked him to take me out tonight, but he insisted on having dinner at home—his favorite dinner, which I hate.

Meatloaf.

And not the singer. *I'd have that Meat Loaf any day.*

I don't even know why I'm so... disgruntled. I doubt he even knows I hate meatloaf.

I should be brimming with excitement, wondering what he got me and where he was taking me. Instead, I'm picking up his dirty laundry and cooking. Like I do every day.

Shaking myself, I shut away all those thoughts.

I do love my husband.

But I regret letting him talk me into being a homemaker. It almost felt fun at first, but quickly soured.

Now it's five years later, and I don't know what I'm doing with my life. I want a career, but I don't even know where to start. Every time I bring up finding a job or even taking a creative writing class, he kills that idea.

But one good thing to come out of this are my dirty little books. I even make money off of them. Not enough to live on, but enough to build me a nice little nest egg. Trevor doesn't know about my books. Or my savings account. The one time I brought up writing and publishing stories, he told me to stop being ridiculous—that there was no way anyone would want to read what I wrote.

I almost let that stop me, but I figured that if I did it under a pen name, it wouldn't matter if they flopped. At least I was having fun. Now, I have forty-two self-published novellas, all smutty and insta-lovey. Silly, fun, short books.

I love to imagine myself living the lives of my heroines. Handsome men ravaging me on the beach, too enthralled to keep their hands off me. Dancing in the rain with a man that adores me.

The men's faces are always hidden, but they aren't Trevor. Another wave of guilt hits me, but I can't help it. I can't see him in any of my heroes.

My phone rings, startling me out of my melancholy.

"Hey, Momma."

"Hey, baby. Tonight's the big night. Where's Trevor taking you?" Mom asks.

"Nowhere. He wants to have a nice dinner at home. So now I have to cook meatloaf," I grumble.

"How very *Rocky Horror* of you."

I laugh. "Oh my goodness."

"I'm sorry, baby. He's such a twerp."

"Mom! He's tired from working so much, and you know he loves meatloaf," I say.

"But it's your anniversary too. Why should you cook something that you don't even like?"

Sighing, I say, "I know. But it's a tough time right now, with him trying to get that promotion."

"Okay, baby. I'm sure it is."

We chat about lighter topics for the next hour, and when we finally hang up, it's time to start dinner.

***

"Bethy, I'm home!" Trevor yells as he walks through the door—an hour late. The meatloaf has dried out, and the vegetables are cold. Some damn anniversary.

I blot my tears and touch up my makeup before I walk into the dining room, fully set for a romantic evening.

"You're late."

"I stopped by my mom's house. She needed me to change a lightbulb."

I mentally roll my eyes. To keep from fighting on our anniversary, I fix him and myself plates and carry them into the dining room.

"How was your day?" I ask, setting his plate in front of him.

"My boss is a fucking asshole. That's how it went," he replies, taking a bite of meatloaf.

"Jeff? I thought you liked Jeff."

He rolls his eyes at me. "Not Jeff, fucking Bennett Sterling. The owner. This meatloaf is a little dry, babe. Did you do something different? I hate when you change things up."

I rub the back of my neck, heat prickling under my skin. "Same recipe. You were an hour late, so it dried out."

"Why do you always have to complain? Can't we have a nice dinner?"

Yes... can't we have a nice dinner?

"I wasn't complaining. I was just stating a fact."

"Of course you were. You know, it's always something with you." He huffs, shoulders slumping.

Feeling guilty, I chip off yet another piece of my pride to have a nice dinner. "I'm sorry. You're right."

He doesn't respond but shoves another bite of meatloaf in his mouth. As he chews, food rolling around his mouth, he says, "Right. So we talked about having a baby after our fifth anniversary, and here we are."

I don't want to have a baby with you.

"You want to have a baby?" *Please say no.*

"You're thirty. Already gaining weight. If you pop the kid out soon enough, maybe you can drop the weight—plus some extra."

"I've only gained like ten pounds. I haven't even changed clothing sizes."

I've been pleasantly plump my entire life. Ten pounds doesn't make one bit of a difference.

The food on the plate has lost any appeal it ever had.

"Yeah, it's so obvious. Maybe you could use this opportunity to get some grown-up clothes—something that looks like it's from this decade would be great. But that's not even the point."

"What *is* the point, Trevor?"

"You know I love you, right? You're a good wife, but I think I need an open marriage. I want an open marriage."

My heart drops into the center of the earth. I'm numb and achy at the same time.

What the did he say to me?

"What?" I ask, unable to process what he said.

He checks his phone and huffs. "I can't be expected to want to fuck you while you get fat. This works out perfectly. You get your baby, and I can still meet my needs. You get it, you've always been practical. It's not like I would fall in love or anything. You'll still be my wife. And if you get in shape, I won't even need to see other women."

Fuck no, you piece of shit.

I'm going to vomit.

Heart pounding, I say, "Okay. Whatever you want."

What the hell, you dumb bitch?

"Great." He checks his phone again. "I'm going to meet up with Paige, a woman I work with. She's the one who suggested the open marriage. Don't wait up. I'll probably sleep in the basement tonight."

Kill him. Serve his mother his head on a platter.

He kisses my temple absentmindedly, grabs his keys, and walks out the door.

I can't breathe. I can't think.

Numbly, I gather our dirty dishes and place them in the sink. I can't even comprehend what happened, what I agreed to.

Tears fill my eyes as I scrub the meatloaf pan like it's his face. Like if I scrub hard enough, I'll erase tonight.

What happened to us? We were so happy.

Weren't we? Were we ever?

I'm sure this is something he only thinks he wants. He won't sleep with another woman—he loves me.

Oh my god. *Oh my god.*

I start sobbing, wrecked by what should have been—glad he isn't here to see what he's done to me. I crawl into our bed on our anniversary and cry myself to sleep. Alone.

Two

Betty

THE FRONT DOOR ALARM chimes, waking me up and letting me know that my husband has come home. I roll over to look at the clock on my bedside table—it's 2 a.m. He's barely been home in the month since he decided to open our marriage. Paige takes up all of his time now, but I find that the less I see of him, the less I want to see of him.

I moved into the guest bedroom three nights after our anniversary dinner. I found that I couldn't bear sharing a bed with him, not now.

He's rummaging in the kitchen, no doubt looking for the dinner that I made earlier. At first, I was hurt that he couldn't even bother to have dinner with me, his wife, before going out with his girlfriend. But those dinners are so uncomfortable, I have nothing to say to him. It's a relief every night that I eat alone.

The sharp shatter of glass and feminine giggles floats up to me. Did he bring another woman into *our* home?

Our fucking *home?*

I fling back the covers and throw on my robe, intending to... I don't know. Yell at him for being disrespectful, or tell them to leave. Something.

I slip down the stairs and look into the kitchen. Some perky redhead sits on *my* counter, giggling while he cleans the glass.

And like the glass, something inside of me shatters.

I remember that move. On our first night in this house, five years ago, I dropped a glass and he picked me up and put me on the counter, so concerned that I would cut my feet. Now he does that for other women. In *my* kitchen.

My goddamn kitchen, where I have cooked his meals for our entire marriage.

A slow, cold rage rolls up my spine.

Two can play this game.

***

Bird&Bee—what a ridiculous name—has been on my phone for twelve hours, and I already have twenty-eight interested men. That boosts my ego. But I've set up a date with one of them, and that has me down. I didn't get married to date other men. What part of 'forsaking all others' did my stupid husband not get?

I need to go to a place where I can clear my head and feel like myself for a little while.

The thrift store.

I shoot a text to my mom, hoping she can meet me there.

I need to tell her about Trevor.

I'm embarrassed, hurt, and disappointed. And I have to tell my mom that I'm going on a date with a man that I'm not married to.

***

The stale scent of dust and old books permeates the air, comforting in its familiarity. Trevor hates thrift stores, thinking that they make him look poor if his wife shops at one. Little does he know, most of our decor is from this exact store—I tell him that I found it at an antique shop.

I go straight to the books, as I always do, knowing my mom will look here first.

Oh my god. Wait. No way.

They have a beautiful Jane Austen set with full-color artwork and all. These are definitely coming with me. I have a whole collection of Austen's works, all sorts of covers and illustrations. These will be a beautiful addition.

It's hard to imagine my life crumbling while there are such fun things in the world. I need to keep reminding myself of this.

I take a glance around and then open the copy of *Pride and Prejudice*, bringing it to my nose. Ah, the scent of old books—I wish I could bottle it.

"I saw that," my mom says from behind, startling me.

I slam the book shut. "Dang it, Mom."

She laughs as she reaches into my cart to pull out *Emma* and flip through. "Oh, this one is lovely. Your collection needs these."

"Right?"

"How are you doing, baby? How's the twerp?" my mom asks, pulling me in for a hug.

I don't say anything. I let my mom hold me. I haven't told my family what is going on. I've needed to think it out alone.

Ma pulls back and looks at me. "Alright, then. Dish."

"Mom, it is so bad."

"I know."

"Long story short? I accidentally agreed to an open marriage and now I have to date again," I say in one long breath, humiliation radiating over my skin.

"Jesus Christ on a cranberry cracker, that was stupid." Mom rolls her eyes.

"Mom! I'm not stupid." I pout, pushing the cart toward the dress rack.

"Of course, you aren't stupid. I don't raise stupid kids. But agreeing to an open marriage when you don't want one is a stupid decision, and you know it. Now, give me the details, and then we'll figure out what to do about this shit show."

I flip through the dresses as I tell my mom about the aftermath of that anniversary dinner.

"That sucks, Honey Bunches of Betties, but the big question is—do you even want it to work out with that twerp?"

"I downloaded that dating app. The bee one," I say.

"Good for you. Now answer the question. Do you want your marriage to work out?"

"I don't know," I whine.

"Yes, you do. Do you want to stay with a man who did that to you?"

"Well, no, of course not, not when you put it like that."

"How else *should* I put it?" Mom raises an eyebrow.

I shrug and pull a red dress off the long rack. "Mom! Look at this one!"

She chuckles. "Great change of subject, but that dress is perfect for you."

"Look, I know my marriage is over. I'm just not ready to file for divorce. Not just yet. I want to make him jealous a little bit."

"That's my girl. Give him hell, but leave with your head held high."

"Too late for that," I reply.

"How so?" Mom asks, pulling a cherry-printed rockabilly dress to hand to me.

I yank it from her. "I need to go play the lottery because I am having all the luck today! Well, except for my unfortunate husband situation. That still sucks."

"Does it, though? He's such a twerp."

"Yeah, yeah. Let's go look at the furniture since I'll be needing to furnish an apartment soon."

"Good girl," Mom says.

We pick our way through until we reach the furniture section. And there it is—my dream bed. Like a beacon of fucking hope.

It's a queen-sized daybed with an intricate white metal frame. Straight out of an old romance novel, it's made for a frilly floral bedspread. I love it so much.

"Mom."

"I see it, Pigeon. Let me call your dad to come pick it up."

"Thanks," I say absently, running my fingers over the cold metal, images of a future without Trevor flashing through my mind.

I'll get to decorate for pleasure and not to show off to others.

A tingle of excitement ripples through my heart. A home where I can openly decorate rather than smuggling a bit of my personality into a cold, sterile house.

"Alright, your dad and Danny will grab it this evening after work. Where do you want them to take it? Our house, your old bedroom?"

"No, no. Um, maybe a storage place? I don't want to clutter up your craft room."

"It was your room first. Hell, your dad still calls it your room," my mom says, flipping through a box of DVDs.

"I know, but I'm not moving in with you guys. I'll be getting my own place, so no reason to move all of your stuff around."

"Fair enough, Betty Bunches. Alright, are we done here? I need to run by the beauty supply store, if you want to ride?"

"Yes! I need to re-do my hair before my date."

***

I dump my haul all over the bathroom counter. I hate how time-consuming maintaining red hair is, but I do so love the outcome. Thanks to my natural blonde roots, it looks like I'm balding if I don't dye it every six weeks. But even though I'm blonde, I still have to bleach it for the red to stick. It's quite the process and turns the tiny room into a bloodbath.

I set up my tablet with a movie and start mixing my bleach. Stir, stir, stir. I should start paying someone to do this, but I don't love strangers touching me, so I do my nails and hair at home.

I'm finishing up, checking all over to make sure I didn't miss any spots, when I hear the front door open.

Damn it. I was hoping he'd work late. Or go see his girlfriend. *Or disappear.*

"Bethany! What's for dinner?" he yells down the hall, as if I care what he eats. If I don't get the perks of being a wife, like his fidelity, then he doesn't get the benefits of being a husband.

"Not shit," I say, as he steps into our bathroom, undoing his tie.

"Why not?" he asks, curling his lip as he looks at my bleach-covered head.

"Because you brought another woman into my kitchen last night," I snap.

"Oh, grow up. Maybe if you didn't dye your hair like a damn teenager, I wouldn't have to go out with more natural women." Trevor stomps away.

The dig lands as he intended. I was never insecure until we got married, and he found fault in everything I did. Once upon a time, Trevor told me that he loved how vibrant and free-spirited I was. He loved my style and dyed hair. Until he didn't. Then I was too bright, too sexy, too colorful, too loud, and everything else I loved about myself. I tried not to change, but I know I've lost some of my shine over the years.

I sigh and check the timer—ten minutes left before I need to wash out the bleach. Then comes the dye. I hope he decides to leave. I don't want to be trapped in this house with him being an asshole.

Speaking of the asshole, he pokes his head in the bathroom and smirks. "Since you don't want to have dinner together, I'm going out."

Tears fill my eyes as the front door slams shut. I'm baffled by this betrayal. He had me fooled. The two years we had together before getting married were so special. He was attentive, complimentary, and kind. We didn't have a fiery, passionate love affair, but a sweet and gentle relationship. I yearn for the passion that I write about, but settled for comfort. Somewhere along the way, things changed so slowly that I never noticed how badly he treated me.

I sit on the toilet and cry.

I cry for the teenager in me who wants a romance novel kind of life.

I cry for the little girl who thought all marriages were fairy tales.

And most of all, I cry for who I am today—betrayed by the very man who promised me loyalty and love until the day he died.

***

"You wanna go shopping with me?" I ask.

"No."

"Please?"

"No."

"Yes."

"Fine. But you have to buy me a treat. A good treat. Not just a drink at the gas station."

"Deal," I tell Danny before tossing my balled-up burger wrapper at his face.

He throws it back at me, but I catch it and stick my tongue out at him.

"Children! Not at the table!" Mom says, chuckling.

My mom demanded that Danny and I show up for lunch. She does this occasionally—being an empty-nester is not for her. She still hasn't forgiven us for moving out.

"Are you coming with us?" I ask my mom—she loves a good shopping trip.

"Can't today, Honey Bunches of Betties. I have a shift at the library."

"Boo. Damn kids," Danny interjects.

"Oh, shush. You guys abandoned me, so I had to go find new kids to hang out with."

"We didn't abandon you! We still come running every time you call!" I reply, laughing.

"You moved out! If that's not abandonment, I don't know what is!" she wails, throwing her hands up.

***

"No, no, no, please, no," Danny whines as we pull into my favorite rockabilly clothing shop.

"Shut up."

"No, seriously. The old ladies in here won't leave me alone."

"It's because you're so dang cute," I laugh, pinching his cheek.

"Shut up."

Danny hops out of my beloved red 1975 VW Rabbit—one of my few rebellions in my marriage. I bought her in my senior year of college, against Trevor's wishes. As soon as we got married, he told me to sell the car. He thought it was an embarrassment. It caused a huge fight when I refused, and I almost gave in. I'm glad I didn't. That would have left me completely dependent on my husband.

We go through the bright yellow door of *Little Miss Rockabilly*. Thelma, the 70-year-old store owner, immediately greets us.

"Betty! You brought us your cutie-pie brother! We should give you a discount for the eye candy."

"You really should!" I laugh, flipping through their newest dresses.

"Why am I here?" Danny complains.

I shrug. "I don't want to be alone right now."

"Yeah, Mom said something was up with you and the twerp. Wanna tell me about it?"

"I do. But after I pick out a dress, then I'll take you out for a coffee and tell you about this bullshit."

"I want a better treat than just coffee," Danny says.

"Boba?"

"Well, yeah. But something else, too. Like a double treat or something."

"Of course. I might even get you three treats today."

"I love having a big sister." Danny chuckles, pulling out dresses in my favorite colors.

"I love that one, but not for tonight." I point at the casual blue dress in his hand.

"What are you doing tonight?"

"That's part of the bullshit with Trevor."

"Boo. Hurry up, then. I need to know."

"Shut up and have some patience." I snicker.

"You shut up."

We browse the dresses, with him pulling more and more inappropriate outfits and me giggling uncontrollably. Danny and I have a nine-year age difference, so he is used to me dragging him shopping with the promise of a treat. He's a senior in college, almost has a teaching degree, but when we get together, he might as well be twelve to my twenty-one again.

Finally, I find *The Dress*. The dress that will make my husband lose his shit. It's pink, sexy, and perfect.

"This is it!"

"Finally! We've been here for years," Danny whines.

"Oh, shush. It's been like twenty minutes. I shouldn't even get you a treat for this."

"You promised!"

***

I take Danny to his favorite cafe and buy him all of the treats he desires. Today, that consists of a taro boba, ham sandwich, and cheesecake for dessert. Once we've settled at a table, Danny looks at me with his eyebrow raised.

"I have a date tonight."

"I guess I'm glad that the twerp is taking you out, but there is no way in hell this is newsworthy," Danny says.

"I don't have a date with Trevor tonight."

Danny freezes, straw in his mouth. "What?"

"Yeah."

"Pigeon, tell me a story—the one about how my married sister ends up going on a date with a man that isn't her husband."

"Well, when your married sister has a worthless husband that asks for an open marriage on their fifth anniversary and then leaves for a date with the new girlfriend, yeah, she ends up going on a date with a man that isn't her husband."

"That son of a bitch," Danny snarls.

"Yeah."

"Your anniversary was weeks ago. *Weeks!* You've been dealing with this bullshit on your own for weeks?"

"I just, I don't know. I had to process, I guess. I just couldn't wrap my mind around this actually happening to me, you know?"

"Yeah, I get that. But next time come to me, or Mom, or even Dad, let us help you process. I don't like thinking about you dealing with this bullshit alone," Danny says, still angry.

"Well, I hope not to have a next time," I say with a giggle.

"Ain't that the truth."

We sit in silence for a little bit while Danny ponders my situation and eats his food. I can see the gears turning in his head.

"So, you're going on a date, but you aren't leaving the asshole?" Danny asks, narrowing his eyes at me.

"I know my marriage is over. I *know* that, but I don't know. I want to hurt him. I want him to feel just a little bit of the betrayal that I feel, you know? I want him to see me going out or coming home the next morning. Both, hopefully."

He sighs. "I don't know, Pigeon. I just want you away from the twerp. God, he's such a piece of shit!"

"Yeah, he is. I just, I don't know. I just need to get a little bit of my pride back. Like, who am I? Just agreeing to an open marriage? I didn't argue or tell him to go to hell or anything. Just agreed."

"Alright then. Let me know how I can help. Anything to screw with that motherfucker," Danny says, finishing off his sandwich. "If I see him, I'm going to punch him, though."

Three

Betty

"WHY ARE YOU ALL dressed up?" Trevor asks, glaring at my reflection in the full-length mirror.

I'm wearing my snazzy new hot pink halter wiggle dress with matching heels and lipstick. My hair is swept up in big, loose curls. A smile tugs on my lips at his question. This is going to be fun.

"I have a date tonight," I say, sliding in my earring.

"No, the hell you do not!"

"Of course, I do. I just spoke with him an hour ago to confirm."

"What the actual fuck, Bethany? How in the hell does my wife have a fucking date?" he snarls at me.

"The same way that my husband has been taking another woman on dates."

"That isn't the same thing, and you know it!"

"This is what you wanted, dear," I say sweetly, batting my eyelashes up at him.

"You being a whore? How is that what I wanted?"

I force myself to keep the smile on my face. "You wanted an open marriage. That implies that we both see other people. Besides, you've really let yourself go since we've gotten married, and I have needs."

The shock on his face is absolutely priceless.

"Whatever, pink looks like shit on you anyways."

I ignore the sinking in my gut, determined to enjoy myself tonight.

Smiling brightly, I grab my pink handbag and say, "Well, regardless, don't wait up. I won't be home tonight."

***

My date, Will, is waiting for me outside Sydney's Bar. He's an alright-looking guy with blonde hair and a dark suit.

I rush up to him. "I'm so sorry I'm late! I—"

"It's fine. Let's go inside," he interrupts me.

I don't like that.

But I follow him inside anyway. I *was* late, he has every right to be perturbed. He walks straight to the bar, not even checking to see if I'm following, and has a seat. I shimmy onto the barstool next to him, no easy feat wearing a tight dress.

"So, what kind of law do you do?" I ask him after a few minutes of awkward silence.

He sighs, still trying to get the bartender's attention, and says, "Family."

"Oh, and do you enjoy that?" I continue, trying to get a conversation going.

Another huff, another look down at the bartender, and another curt answer. "It's fine."

"Well, that's nice."

This feels like a less comfortable date with Trevor, short answers and all.

The bartender moseys over to us with a huge smile on her lovely face. Will sneers and says, "About time. I want a beer and get my date whatever."

I bristle at his rough treatment of this lady, who takes his douchebaggery in stride.

I glance at her nametag. "Hey, Sarah, I'd like a lemon drop martini, please."

"Right away," she replies.

Glancing over at Will, I find him leering at me. I smile uncomfortably, wishing that the date was over.

"So, an open marriage, huh? You must be wild in the sack."

Startled and regretting my honesty on that stupid app, I smile uncomfortably at him. "So what do you do for fun?"

"Hopefully you," he says, still staring at me.

"I, uh, no. No, no thanks," I stammer out.

His face turns red, rage flashing in his eyes. "Stupid slut, wouldn't fuck you if you begged for it."

I jolt back, shock keeping me silent.

He chugs his beer, slams the bottle on the counter, and stomps to the restroom with one last glare at me.

Well, that was abrupt. And mean. Who even talks to a stranger like that?

I make eye contact with the bartender, who shrugs her shoulder and says, "I'd leave while he's in that bathroom. Save yourself some grief."

I can leave.

With that thought bouncing around my head, I glance towards the restrooms, checking for Will, before rushing out the door. I hustle to my car, hoping he doesn't try to catch up to me, and quickly drive out of the parking lot.

Unsure of where to go, I drive to my favorite little town, Verbania. I park at L'albergo Verbania and stare at the beautifully ornate hotel, wishing I had an occasion to stay there. Trevor didn't see any need to stay a mere hour away from our house, but I've always dreamed of a romantic night in the hotel.

Screw it.

I'm going to treat *myself* to a romantic night at the hotel.

I used to think that this hotel would be perfect for anniversaries. Perhaps it is. But maybe it's also the perfect place to start over. Alone.

***

"Welcome to L'albergo Verbania, Mrs. Miller."

"Actually, it's Ms. Miller."

"My apologies, Ms. Miller, Anthony here will show you to your room." Lilith says, tucking her pink hair behind an ear.

Am I really doing this? Staying at my dream hotel, alone?

Yes. Yes, I am.

"Thank you."

"Right this way, ma'am. Are you here for business or fun?" Anthony asks as we board the elevator.

"Fun. My husband is a scumbag and I'm letting him think I'm out screwing other guys."

"Oh my god. That sounds hilarious, not the scumbag husband part, of course. But the revenge part. Please call the front desk and ask for me if you need any help. Like a dude voice in the background of a call! Please!" Anthony chirps, practically vibrating with excitement.

I can't help but laugh, my previously dampened spirits brightened again.

"Oh, I most definitely will! Thank you," I say as we leave the elevator and go to my hotel room.

"You're welcome. I hope your stay is as fun as it sounds!"

***

My favorite movie is playing on the TV, and my Mediterranean food is spread out on the bed in front of me. I take another bite of hummus with pita bread, feeling at peace for the first time in weeks.

I do not love my husband anymore. I don't think I have in a long time, this open marriage deal forced me to accept it much earlier than I would have on my own. I try to be thankful that my husband asked my permission to cheat on me instead of doing it behind my back for years.

But I'm still too angry.

One day, I'm sure I'll be grateful. Grateful that we didn't have a child together and that I only wasted seven years with him.

But that day is not today. I want revenge.

Not a big revenge. Just a little one.

My phone dings, alerting me to a text message. Then another, and another. I dig my phone out of the covers and see message after message pour in. They're all from Trevor, ranging from "Baby, I miss you" all the way to "Fuck you," and everything in between. My thumb hovers over the screen, wanting to reply. But what can I even say?

What's left to say?

Knowing that nothing will save a marriage that neither of us want to save, I block my husband's number. Severing one tie to him, even though we still live in the same house. Tonight is the first time he's texted me in weeks, too busy with his girlfriend to worry about his wife. Until his wife starts dating, of course.

Well, fuck him.

I hope this makes him so jealous that he can't stand it. This evening proves that I'm not ready to date, yet, but he doesn't need to know that. I'll take myself out on dates and end the night in my hotel room. And then I will make sure that I go home still wearing the same thing that I left in.

With that thought, I climb out of bed, grab my lovely pink dress from the closet, and ball it up before I toss it on the floor. It hurts to treat a dress this way, but I need it crumpled. I want it to look like a man was barely able to control himself around me.

Sighing, I climb back into the bed, almost sending the falafel rolling. Not that any man has ever wanted me so badly he couldn't control himself. But I deserve passion, don't I? I deserve to have what I give the heroines in my books. Love, passion, affection, and devotion. I want it. I kept hoping that Trevor would give it to me, but how is an open marriage the precursor to any of it? It isn't.

***

I time my arrival back at the house that Trevor and I share—I can't call it my home anymore—to coincide with him leaving for work. I want him to see me in my rumpled dress, but I don't want to spend any amount of time with him.

I unlock and open the door, nervous about what I'll find.

Trevor is pacing the living room, eyes bloodshot, reeking of booze, and his hair looks like he's been pulling on it. The urge to run away hits me like a train, I've never seen him so disheveled.

"Where the fuck have you been?" Trevor yells from across the room.

My heart races. My eyes burn. Damn it. I take a deep breath and release it, begging my heart rate to slow. Panic races through my veins, I expected jealous, not furious.

Please don't notice my shaking hands.

"You knew I was going on a date. Where have *you* been? You look like shit," I reply, thrilled that my voice isn't trembling.

"Where have I been? Where the fuck have I been? I've been at this goddamn house. Waiting for you!" he shouts, running his hands through his hair.

Welcome to my world, motherfucker.

"Oh, well, that is unfortunate. I had a lovely time, but I'm exhausted. I think I'll take a bath and a nap. Shouldn't you go on to work?"

"Fuck you."

I smirk, shrug, and walk right past him and up the stairs to the bedroom. The front door slams, and I watch from the window as he peels out of the driveway.

When his car vanishes from view, I let the tears roll down my face. My whole body shakes as the adrenaline rushes from my veins.

I should feel good—triumphant even—but I'm just sad.

Sobs rack my body as I collapse on the bed. I can't catch my breath, the room is too small. I don't want this. All I ever wanted was a cute little life. Someone to love and a job that doesn't suck. My family and date nights.

And a loyal husband.

I wish I had never married him. *Never met him.*

***

"That son of a bitch. What'd he say after that?" Danny glares at me from the couch.

"He slammed his empty beer bottle down and went to the restroom, I think. I don't know. I left."

"Why'd you stay so long? You should have walked away when he was snippy about you being late."

A wave of realization washes over me. *I should have walked away.* I should have walked away from Trevor years ago. I should have walked away from Will as soon as he showed his asshole side. I've wasted too much time on men who don't deserve it.

"I just, it just never occurred to me that I could leave, I guess. I was so used to Trevor and being unhappy that I didn't think about it."

"Maybe you should stop that shit," Danny says.

"Shut up." I laugh, throwing a piece of popcorn at him.

He smirks at me after catching the popcorn with his mouth. We are lying on the sofas in my parents' basement watching a movie on their huge TV. Danny and I try to do a movie night a couple of times a month.

Usually, our parents join us, but we caught them on the way out the door for date night. I can't even remember the last time that Trevor took me out for a date.

Not that it matters anymore.

"Why don't you just move in with Mom and Dad? Or you could stay with me, but I doubt you want an air mattress on a dorm room floor," Danny says, his face serious.

"Why would I do that?"

Danny makes an annoyed sound. "To get away from the twerp! Jesus, Pigeon. He was yelling at you! You need to get out of that house. Let us take care of you until you get on your feet—just leave him!"

"I can get my own place. I'm just not ready to yet."

"Not to be that guy but how can you afford to get a place when you haven't worked since you got married?"

Giggling, I can't decide how to tell my baby brother that I make money writing smut.

"Do you want the 'nice to meet you' version or the real story?"

"Dear Lord. Both. Give me both," he groans.

"I write romance short stories and sell them on the Sterling app."

"That doesn't sound too bad," he says, tentatively.

"Yeah, well, they're actually mostly smut."

"Smut? Like, sex books? You write *porn*?" Danny looks horrified.

I lift my shoulders. "Pretty much. They sell really well, too."

"What name do you write under? I need to make sure I never even accidentally read one of your books," Danny says, laughing and making gagging faces.

"Tilda Vaughn."

"Nice name," Danny mumbles, typing away on his phone. "Damn, you have a shit-ton of books on here!"

"Yeah, I've been writing them for four years. I thought you wanted to avoid them, not look them up."

"I'm just curious. *The Matchmaker's Menage*? *Werewolves Love Busty Blondes*? Seriously?" Danny chuckles.

"Oh, shut up. Those are two of my best sellers!"

"Damn, I see that. Well, good for you, Pigeon. I'm pretty grossed out, but this is really cool. You always did want to be a writer."

"I did, I do. I mean, this isn't really writing, you know. Just little stories."

"Well, Sterling has you listed as an author. You have forty-two books listed under your pen name. These books have mostly four and five-star reviews. I think that makes you a writer, Pigeon."

Damn, my stupid brother sees me more clearly than my husband ever did.

My eyes fill with tears, and I turn to focus on whatever movie Danny picked for tonight. Something about an underdog sports team winning against all odds or similar. Blinking rapidly, I look up, but it doesn't work. The tears fall down my face.

"I'm not hugging you!" Danny exclaims, throwing a box of tissues at me.

"I don't want your stupid hugs anyways." I sniffle.

Four

Betty

"Damn it!" I snap at myself as I try to get my hair to lie right.

I'm following a video tutorial on how to do a high ponytail with a victory roll, but it's not going well. I try again, twisting my hair and inserting a bobby pin. Now the moment of truth—when I let go, will it stay rolled? I let go and... no. No, it didn't stay rolled. I release a long breath and brush out my cherry red hair, pull it into a regular high ponytail, and throw a hot pink ribbon around it.

I check my outfit in the full-length mirror: pink pedal pushers, black wedges, and a black Rob Zombie band tee that I've tied under my tits, showing some of my soft stomach skin. I add a pink lipstick that matches the pants and grab my black bag. Perfect! I'm so excited for today. I'm taking myself out for ice cream and a trip to the bookshop. Then I'm going to stay at L'albergo Verbania and order greasy take-out to eat in bed while watching a fun movie. This whole dating myself thing is way better than dating Trevor ever was.

I skip down the hall when I hear the front door open. Oh, goodie. Trevor is here to see me off on my date.

"Where are you going in such a good mood?" he snarls at me.

"I have a day date! He's taking me out for ice cream!"

"Has he seen you? You don't need any more ice cream."

"Oh, he's seen me alright," I laugh, watching him slowly unravel.

"What the fuck is that supposed to mean? Are you fucking him?"

What an idiot.

I shrug and smirk at him. "It's not polite to kiss and tell."

His face turns so red I become concerned for his health.

Not concerned enough to check on him, but concerned. I grab my keys from the bowl and walk right out the door, leaving him sweating and sputtering.

***

Back in Verbania, I can breathe again. It's so cute here, full of small businesses, and the center of the town is very walkable.

Trevor hates it. Which is perfect—no chance of running into him.

I park in the big public lot outside of the town circle and stroll to Verbania Sweets and Treats, pulling open the teal door to a candy wonderland. Willy Wonka would be jealous, and I love it so much. Oversized candy replicas decorate the walls, silly contraptions display sweets, and lively circus music creates an atmosphere of whimsy.

After poking around for twenty minutes, I get in line for an ice cream cone, dancing in place. I haven't felt this carefree, this me, in a long time.

There is a young man in front of me holding the hand of a toddler. He turns and looks me up and down before smirking at me. "Rob Zombie, huh? Can you even name three songs of his?"

I roll my eyes and reply, "Yep."

He looks at me expectantly. "Well?"

"Well, what?" I ask.

"Thought you were going to name some Rob Zombie songs."

"I said I could, not that I would. I don't have shit to prove to you."

That shuts him up.

A cute little teenager takes my order, and all unpleasantness is forgotten. I take my cotton candy ice cream with pink sprinkles outside and roam the town, peeking into shop windows until my cone is gone.

I meander over to the huge bookshop, Enchanted Verbania, and walk into one of the most accurately named businesses ever. This place is pretty darn enchanting with twinkle lights, whimsical art, and books galore.

I head straight for the romance, loving all the bright and fun covers, and start browsing. I get lost in the world of romance and whimsy, and then my arms are full of books. Must be time to check out.

Holy hot Thor—look at the fellow at the cash register. I roll my tongue back into my mouth, pick my jaw up off the floor, and place my books on the counter. He smiles at me as he totals my purchases, his bright blue eyes crinkling in the corners, and hands me my bag of books.

I make it to the door when an idea forms and I backtrack to Thor.

"Excuse me, could I speak with your manager, if they aren't busy?"

"I'm one of the owners, Fable Ashford at your service," he says.

"Betty Miller, pleased to meet you," I reply, shaking his hand. "I won't take up much of your time. But do you have any job openings?"

"As a matter of fact we do! Do you have time for a chat? We actually have an immediate need for a bookseller," he says with a kind smile.

He leads me to a little chair grouping in view of the cash register and door. As we sit down he continues, "Hope you don't mind having our chat out here. I have to keep an eye on the register."

"Oh, that's no problem. I worked at a small bookstore in college so I totally get it."

"You're hired!" he says, laughing. "But seriously, we really are in desperate need of another person here. We recently had two employees quit out of nowhere. They were a married couple and had been talking about moving back to their home state for months but instead of telling us when and all that they just left. Did a couple no-call, no-shows until we tracked Jimmy down and found out that they were halfway across the country. So now it's just me and my mom trying to run this joint but we really need more than two people. So tell me about yourself."

"Well, I went to Coslada College and majored in literature while working at Empoli Book Emporium. I was at the Emporium a total of seven years, and managed it for four."

"Why did you leave Empoli?" he asks.

"I got married and became a homemaker. But you won't have to worry about that happening again, and I would never leave you in the lurch."

"Good, good. And you live here in Verbania?"

"No, I live in Coslada."

"That would be a long drive to work," he says skeptically.

My impulsivity gets the better of me and I reply, "I'm in the process of moving over here."

As soon as I say it, a weight lifts from my shoulders. I'm really going to leave my husband and move to Verbania.

"Well, good enough for me. How about we start you off part-time until you move out here and then we can discuss full-time?"

"That would be perfect!" I exclaim, excited about the future that I'm building.

***

I'm so nervous.

I haven't worked outside of that damn house in five years. But this is good.

This is me finally taking my life back.

I'm sitting in my car, parked by the hotel. I couldn't bear the thought of going home and seeing Trevor after this monumental day. So L'albergo Verbania, I'll see you later tonight. I pull down the visor, checking my lipstick and fluffing my hair.

I spent hours figuring out today's outfit. I want to be myself, but also, this is work. I settled right in the middle, with black pedal pushers and a baby-blue boat-neck top. Black loafers and ruffled socks complete the look.

Deep breath, in and out. One last mirror check and I climb out of my little red car.

I trek down the sidewalk and into Enchanted Verbania, finding it almost empty. Thank the universe I can learn the ropes on a slow day. Relieved, I seek out Fable.

"You must be Betty," a sweet voice says from behind me. That voice belongs to a woman who has to be Fable's mother, tall, slender, and strikingly gorgeous. Silver hair falls in a sleek waterfall down her back, and her black sheath dress adds to her simple elegance. "I'm Meredith, Fable's mom."

"So happy to meet you!" I exclaim, shaking her hand.

"Aren't you the cutest little thing. I can just tell you'll fit right in here. Great!" She chatters, not pausing for a breath. She gestures for me to follow her as she continues her monologue. "Let's go find Fable, he's going to be training you today. I've been here all day and you know, I was partly retired until Pam and Jimmy ran off. But no bother. You're here now, and once we get you up to full-time and hire someone else, you don't know anyone looking for a job, do you? I opened this shop some forty years ago, and we've been right here ever since, but Fable runs the show now. He's a good boy, you're going to love working here."

We find hot Thor—I mean Fable—stocking plushies in the children's area. I hadn't ventured in this section last time, so the magic catches me off guard. It's a fairy tale of a room. Shimmering wooden trees, a huge castle made for the kids to play in, and twinkle lights galore. Plush chairs and beanbags are settled in corners, under canopies.

I wish my job was to get cozy and read, because this is so inviting.

"Betty! I see you've met Marmee. Now we can get to training. Shouldn't be anything new to you, just learning our vibe here."

"It's been so long since I've worked at Empoli, you might want to train me like I've never done this before," I say, grimacing, hating Trevor for convincing me to quit.

"I'm sure it's like riding a bike, but either way, we are pretty laid-back and Fable here is a great teacher. You'll be just fine, dear. Now, then, Fable-baby, I'm going to go on home. You take care of our girl, I'll see you later," Meredith rambles before turning to me and pulling me in for a hug. "I hope you don't mind, I'm a hugger. And I just know we are going to be great friends so I figure I shouldn't miss out on a hug just because we haven't become friends yet. You know? Fable, come here and give me a kiss so I can get out of your hair."

Fable smiles at his mother and kisses her cheek, tugging her in for a quick squeeze. She pats his cheek and gives me a wave before disappearing around a bookshelf.

Fable chuckles. "Sorry about Marmee, she's a talker. I bet she asked you twenty questions and didn't let you answer a single one."

"Yup, but I love it. No apologies needed." I laugh.

"Good, good." Fable claps once and continues, "Now, then. Let's get to work. I'm going to train you on the register first thing, then we'll do a tour and go over everything else. Don't worry if it all goes over your head, as long as you can run the register after today, that's the biggest problem we have right now."

"I think I can handle that!" I chirp, following him to the checkout counter.

The rest of the day flies by. I pick up the register quickly, so Fable gets to go stock and help customers while I run the front end. My back hurts from standing on my feet all day, but I feel so good. I have a purpose, and this income is going to ensure that I can afford to leave my husband.

I can leave my husband.

Well, I can leave him after I make him suffer for a little while.

Knowing that I can get away from Trevor whenever I choose is liberating.

Light-hearted, I step next door to grab dinner and stroll to the hotel. I haven't felt this free in years.

Five

Bennett

"Whatcha got going on this weekend?" Stella asks, checking the oven.

"Working, as usual. I have an estate sale to visit on Sunday morning."

"Bennett, can I tell you something? I've said it before, but I think you need to hear it again."

"Oh, um, yes," I stammer, anxiety sliding up my back.

"You're lonely. You need friends, or at least one friend. Or someone to love. Something. All you do is work."

"I'm not lonely. I do not particularly enjoy being around groups of people."

That feels like a lie. I need to write this feeling down in my notebook for further contemplation.

"I'm not saying hit a bar or anything. Just... something. Find something to matter to you. I worry about you, baby."

I'm always amazed at the juxtaposition of Stella being sweet. She is a biker chick in her 50s with bleach-blonde hair and leather pants. I had interviewed seven other ladies to be my housekeeper—she was the last one. Walked right in and informed me that she was exactly who I was looking for and asked when I wanted her to start. And here we are.

That was five years ago, and she is my perfect housekeeper. She keeps my house exactly how I like it, and I enjoy talking to her when our schedules overlap. Even though she is only about fifteen years older than my forty-three years, she mothers me. Hovers around, offering advice and pushing me to get out more. Always shakes her head as if I were a naughty schoolboy when I go to yet another charity ball alone.

"I'm going to an estate sale this weekend. That matters to me." I fix the sleeve of my suit, careful not to look at Stella.

Pulling my Wednesday casserole out of the oven, Stella replies, "But you don't enjoy it. I'm talking about having a good time. When was the last time you had fun, huh?"

That statement hits me in the chest. *I've never had fun.*

***

The driver drops me off in front of a small mansion—ornate in every way—the kind of home that emphasizes the wealth of the owner. I don't often use a driver, but the parking at estate sales is notoriously bad. Even at 7 a.m. on a Sunday. I thought people enjoyed sleeping in.

The house has the musty smell associated with a space that hasn't been aired out in a long time. Usually, this scent accompanies me finding the best vintage books, so that is promising. A couple of elderly ladies stand guard at the door, letting the potential buyers know where everything is. I'm directed to the second floor, third room on the left.

A library. A very well-stocked library.

I assess the shelves, noticing quite a few books that I don't have in my collection, until I find what I came for.

The encyclopedias.

Three sets. Vintage. Perfect condition.

My heart pounds. There it is: the *Velona Traditional Encyclopedia*, from 1803. Only about ten full sets remain from the original run of fifty. This one, in particular, is special—not only because of its rarity, but because of its color: a lovely purple.

The purple dye came from sea snail secretion, making it a prized luxury among the wealthy. Of course, the *Velona Printing Press* went out of business after making such an outrageously expensive color choice for encyclopedias.

I have been searching for this set my whole life. In fact, when my parents had the nanny find out my birthday wishes, this set has been at the top since I was five.

Voices on the stairs interrupt my musings. A group of young women enter the room and immediately my pleasure dissipates. I pretend to browse the shelves above the encyclopedias, unwilling to leave them unattended with so many people around. Luckily, the group seems to prefer the modern classics that line the other side of the room.

"Excuse me, could you grab that book on the top shelf for us? We are but poor petite ladies and require a big strong man," one of the women says, all of the ladies giggling.

"Yes," I reply, stepping around the girl. "Which book in partic- ular?"

"Oh, um, that one... um, the red one," the girl stammers, sound- ing unsure.

I've said something wrong.

I hover beside the shelf, one eye on the prized set and one on the girls now giggling in a corner. I've waited most of my life for this encyclopedia. But now all I can think about is how loud this room has become. I don't belong here. Not with them. Not in this moment.

I need to leave.

I grab the book and hand it to her before glancing back at the encyclopedias.

I make my way down the stairs as quickly as possible, without drawing attention, done with this excursion. I barely remember paying for my encyclopedias or calling my driver to help me load them. I'm restless after that encounter. I'll have to go to the gym this afternoon, or I won't be able to sleep tonight.

In the car, touching my newest prized possession, I wonder: *Was that fun?*

***

In the fluorescently lit locker room, with the sounds of people laughing, showering, and clanging metal, it's hard to hear myself think. I always hate the necessity of using this room smelling of disinfectant and body odor. But I cannot very well walk down the street looking like I got into a round of fisticuffs.

"Hey, man, good sparring with you today."

Startled, I respond. "You as well."

Todd, as he was introduced before our session, smiles at me and asks, "Me and my buddies are watching the fight this weekend. You want to meet us up at that sports bar on Fifth?"

I hate sports bars.

"No, thank you," I reply, unwrapping my hand.

"Oh, alright. Maybe I'll see you around, then."

"Yes. I'm here five days a week, two of those days for MMA."

"Cool, man." Confusion shows clearly on Todd's face as he walks away.

That was an incorrect social interaction.

I need to write this down.

I have trained in MMA at this gym twice a week for the last four years. This is the first time anyone has invited me anywhere, or even actually spoken to me. They are all friendly enough, and I have plenty of sparring partners but no one has ever invited me out.

I would have declined anyway.

Walking out of the locker room I spot Todd with a group of men, all laughing. A twinge of—I don't know—loneliness, perhaps, hits me. Do I want to spend time with them? Or with someone? I haven't felt this since childhood.

I think Stella has influenced my thinking.

I rush out of the building, walking rapidly to my apartment, the need to write these feelings down crushing me.

Everything is a blur until I reach my bedroom where I grab my journal and write down what happened.

Finally, I can breathe again. Upon reflection, I believe that I should have invited Todd for a drink at the gym's smoothie bar since I declined the sports bar invitation. People enjoy knowing that their company is wanted.

It is so hard to remember how to interact in social situations.

If only everything came as naturally to me as business does.

Six

Betty

I'M PUTTING THE FINAL touches on my makeup when Trevor gets home. Home—ha. The house that he and I share.

"Bethy!" he yells, using his nickname for me. I thought it was sweet at first, then realized that he used it because he hates that I go by Betty.

"Don't you look hot tonight? Why don't you throw on something nicer, and I'll take you to L'albergo Verbania. I know you've been wanting to go." He's leaning against the doorframe, holding a bouquet of lilacs and peonies. My favorites. His blue tie is loosened, and his sleeves are rolled up, adding to his charm. My traitorous heart skips a beat. Damn it, he knows he looks good like that. This is what I've always wanted from Trevor—romance. *Yes* is on the tip of my tongue. I almost squeal, almost do a stupid little dance.

Luckily, reality slams into me before I do all of that.

He was screwing some other girl last night.

He's only doing this because I went on a date. He doesn't want me, but he doesn't want to lose me. Hell, I wouldn't want to lose the person who waits on me hand and foot, either. Thinks he can throw me a little romance and I'll stay home?

Screw that noise. I always waited on him—never again.

"Sorry, can't! But oh my god! My date tonight is taking me to L'albergo Verbania so you don't even have to! I know how you hate those kinds of places. Are those for me? They're beautiful!" I say all of this while patting him on the cheek and taking the bouquet from his hand. Then I squeeze past him and walk to the kitchen to put them in water. I might be done with the man but the flowers didn't do a damn thing wrong.

He's still sputtering as he walks down the hall, growing agitated as his tiny brain works overtime to figure out what happened.

"What the hell? You're going to ditch me for some loser?"

I laugh. "I'm not ditching you. We didn't have plans."

"I'm your fucking husband!"

"Sure you are. Now, I do have to run. Laters." I say, grabbing my purse and keys. I hustle to the door and make it out before he has a chance to reply.

Thank the universe for small miracles.

***

"Ms. Miller, great to see you again! Your room is ready," Lilith says, tapping a couple buttons on her computer. She is such a cute contradiction, wearing a conservative pantsuit in navy blue, similar to what Anthony is wearing. But from the neck up, she is all elfin features and light pink braids contrasting with her deep brown skin.

"Are we making our husband jealous again?" Anthony whoops, bouncing up to the reception desk.

"Making our husband jealous?" Lilith asks, fascination coating her expression.

"Can I tell her?" Anthony asks, before I can even get a word in.

I giggle. "Go right ahead."

"So, Ms. Va-va-voom here has a sleazy husband, and we're making him think she's out all night with other gentlemen."

"Oh, I love that," Lilith says, leaning over the counter. "What'd he do?"

She glances around and straightens her posture, instantly appearing more professional, and whispers, "If you don't mind me asking, of course."

Anthony is vibrating with excitement at getting more of the story, but another guest walks up, interrupting the fun.

I wiggle my fingers in goodbye and make my way to my hotel room, chuckling to myself.

I intended to have some food delivered and watch a movie in my comfy clothes, but a little drink at the hotel bar sounds nice. I want to be around other people.

After dropping my bag on the bed and touching up my makeup, I meander into the lavish hotel bar.

I feel like everyone is looking at me as I scoot onto the last stool by the wall. Sasha, the bartender, saunters over to me—all smiles and practiced charm. I order a lemon drop martini and settle in to people-watch.

I sip my drink as the patrons come and go, merriment in the air.

I spot Anthony and Lilith giggling at the front desk, so I decide to be brave and make friends.

Anthony calls my name as soon as he sees me, while Lilith gestures for me to join them.

"So, Anthony told me what he knows. Which is practically nothing. I want to know the story here!" Lilith whines playfully as I step up to the counter.

"Be more subtle, gosh," Anthony chirps, slapping Lilith's shoulder.

I chuckle. "It's totally fine. I just don't even know where to start."

A loud crowd bursts in the front doors, gathering around the reception counter, so I know that's my cue to leave.

"Can we have lunch tomorrow? So we can chat uninterrupted?" Lilith asks, patting my hand.

"Of course!"

***

The walk to Wild Rose Mediterranean takes us around the hotel fountain and we stop so I can dig a coin from my bag.

"Here you go," I say, handing Lilith a penny and keeping one for myself. "Let's make a wish."

She giggles and we toss our coins in at the same time.

"What'd you wish for?" she asks me.

"I can't tell you. Obviously."

"Boo."

"Oh shush, you know you won't tell me either."

"Yeah, yeah. So. Tell me everything about this whole husband situation. I'm dying—literally dying—to know the details."

I let out a dramatic groan. "Yeah, my marriage turned into a damn trainwreck."

She nods her head, giving me the space to gather my thoughts. We reach the restaurant and get a table in the back.

We chat about nonsense until our drinks are on the table and the food ordered. I don't know how much to share with my new friend here. My tendency to blab my whole life story to anyone who would listen really annoyed Trevor.

"Look, I know we don't know each other but I'm a great listener. And I can keep a secret," Lilith says, breaking the silence.

I let out a long, weary breath. "Okay, so I married my college sweetheart and like an idiot agreed to be a homemaker. Because he wanted it, not me."

"That sucks. I love my home, I'm such a bed person. But the idea that some man wants me to stay home would piss me off."

"Right? I was mad most of the time but didn't even realize it. We were married for five years. Five damn years, and then on our anniversary he says he wants a baby and an open marriage."

She gasps. "Holy cow. Just... holy cow."

"Yeah, since I'll get fat while pregnant and he has needs, he thinks he should be able to screw other women. I was in shock and agreed." I take a sip of my soda, waiting for her judgment.

"My stars... like, what could you have said? You couldn't be anything other than shocked."

"I know, right? What the actual hell, right? And then tonight, after weeks of him being gone with his girlfriend, he waltzes in, acting all sweet. Reminded me of how he used to be. I almost folded like a cheap lawn chair," I say with a bitter chuckle.

"What a douchebag."

"Tell me about it. So I went on one date and he was a real jerk. I don't want to do that again. So I am dating myself. Taking myself out for ice cream and romantic nights in a hotel." I laugh. "It's so much more fun than it would be with Trevor anyways."

"Oh, no way! That sounds so stinking cute!"

"Thank you! I thought so! And I had always wanted to stay at L'albergo Verbania so after that stupid date I just drove straight there. And here we are!"

"This is going to sound childish but do you want to be friends?" Lilith asks.

Surprised but thrilled, I reply, "Yes! I would love to be friends!"

"Good! I would rather ask and get this shit out of the way instead of wondering if we are actually friends or just friendly, you know? Okay, let's exchange numbers—and do you want to come over to my house and watch a movie tomorrow?" Lilith rambles, handing me her phone open to contacts.

"I love movie nights! Yes, please! Should I bring snacks or maybe dinner?"

"I'm a movies in bed kind of gal, I have snacks. All of the usual movie watching ones, popcorn and the seasonings, candy, beef jerky. Plus a bunch of other stuff. I love junk food." She giggles.

Somehow, watching Lilith laugh, I feel like my old self. The me I was before Trevor crushed my impulsivity under the guise of being mature.

This feels good, really good.

***

I press send on the text telling Lilith that I'll be late—but this time, it's *not* my fault! The hot cowgirl casserole took a little longer to cook than I expected.

Probably because I didn't read the recipe until it was too late. No way to make it *and* be on time. Damn it.

I pull it out of the oven and tuck it into my casserole carrier before dashing into my bedroom to slip my shoes on. A key turns in the lock, damn it, Trevor is home. My stomach clenches. He's early, and I lost track of time again. My heart racing, I snag everything and hustle down the stairs as he gets the front door open.

"Bethy! Something smells good, baby!"

I grab the casserole and beeline for the door. "Thanks, it's for my date! Gotta run, I'm late!"

A quick glance over my shoulder, before the door shuts, shows Trevor standing there with his jaw on the floor.

Once I'm in my car with the doors locked, I finally let out an almost hysterical laugh. It's funny but I'm staying stressed. He's been so irrational and unpredictable since I started dating, I don't know what kind of situation I'll have at home on any given day.

Maybe I'm going too far.

I immediately reject that thought, he went too far when he screwed another woman. I wish I could be more vicious, but it's not me. Seeing movement in the window I quickly throw the car into gear and get on the road to Verbania.

***

"Betty! Come on in!" Lilith says, holding the door to her apartment open so I can scurry inside.

Her front door opens into the kitchen, so I set the dish on her counter before glancing around her small apartment. One word comes to mind when looking around Lilith's home—soft. Covered in pastels and luxe fabrics with plants and twinkle lights everywhere. Her rug looks like it would be amazing to walk on barefoot.

It looks like she loves it here.

"What did you bring us? It smells so good."

"I figured since you were providing the junk food, I'd bring us a casserole for dinner," I reply, unzipping the carrier to show her.

"I'm going to fall in love with you if you aren't careful."

"Maybe that's what I want," I say, tossing her a cheeky wink.

Lilith giggles. "Okay, so you're going to think I'm super gross but how do you feel about grabbing a couple forks and the casserole and eating it in bed?"

"That sounds so cozy! You won't get mad at me if I drop food on your sheets?"

Lilith barks out a laugh. "Goodness, no. I have like twenty sheet sets because I'm always dropping food. And then I have to change the sheets, even if it doesn't make a mess. I can't sleep on dirty sheets."

"I get that! Let's do it!"

Lilith grabs a cute light yellow cooler and scoops ice from her freezer before throwing an assortment of canned sodas in. She points to a basket of snacks and asks me to carry that while she carries the cooler and casserole.

Her bedroom is even more magical than the rest of her home. It feels like you could run, jump, and land anywhere—and it would be cushioned and comfy. The theme of pastels and twinkle lights continues, now featuring a huge bed that wraps the room in comfort and a TV mounted on the wall. It even has one of those cute picture frames around it, making it look like art, almost.

We set our haul in the middle of her bed and climb up.

"Make yourself a nest and we'll dig in. What movie do you want to watch?" Lilith asks, fluffing one of her gazillion pillows and arranging them all around her. I follow suit and find myself so snug that I might never leave.

"How about a comedy? Something silly, I had a little run-in with my husband, and I could use something light-hearted."

"Oh, shit. What happened?"

"Nothing, really. He just came in and said that it smells good as I ran right out the door. I don't know what to expect with him anymore," I say, popping the top of a soda.

Lilith opens the hot dish, hands me a fork, and huffs. "Not to be that guy, but you should totally leave him."

"I know. I am. I just want him to suffer before I go."

"Alrighty-then." She gears up the TV and gets a silly teen cheer-leading movie going. Soon, most of the casserole and all thoughts of my scumbag husband are gone, and Lilith and I are chanting the cheers along with the team.

Seven

Bennett

"Have a good weekend, Mr. Sterling," my receptionist chirps, as I open my office door.

"Thank you. I hope you have a good weekend as well, Ms. Barker."

"Oh, I will! I have a date with my boyfriend!"

Unsure of how to respond, I nod and hurry to the elevator, hoping she's not getting on with me. Being stuck in an elevator with a chatty person is my nightmare.

I always take a left outside the office to walk home, three blocks away. But today I take a right. It feels necessary, but it unsettles me to break routine.

A strange excitement worms its way into my chest. It's been years since I've deviated from my usual path. I slow my walk and look around. I've never explored the area around Sterling Corporation before. I go to work, then home, stopping at the gym, which is exactly halfway between.

I turn a corner and come face-to-face with an animal shelter, a sign in the window declaring *Kittens Half-Price*. I could pay full price for a kitten, but I've never considered owning a pet. It might be nice to have someone excited to see me at the end of the day. Cats *are* independent little creatures. I can afford the care, and Stella is always telling me that I need a friend.

A feline friend sounds ideal—no awkward conversations.

"Good evening, sir. How can I help you?" A chipper girl with blue hair greets me.

"I am considering adopting a cat. May I see the ones you have available?"

"Oh, goodie! Please follow me." She leads me down a hall and into a large room full of kittens and things for kittens to do. I step inside, uncertain, when a tiny white cat, its ears, nose, tail, and paws tipped in gray, latches onto my pant leg and climbs up to my shoulder.

I freeze, my heart pounding. I've never imagined myself in such a situation.

"Aww, looks like someone picked you!" the girl squeals, snapping a picture on her phone. "I'll send this to you!"

"Thank you," I say, lifting the small cat from my shoulder to look at it. If my knowledge of felines is correct, this one is a Siamese.

I immediately decide that this kitten belongs with me.

"I will take this one," I say, placing the cat back on my shoulder.

The girl giggles. "You don't want to meet any of the others?"

"No, thank you. Just this one, please."

"Alrighty then, I have some paperwork for you. You picked a sweet little girl. We've named her Ginger."

"But she isn't orange."

"Yes, well, one of the other girls just really liked the name Ginger."

This cat isn't orange and thus should not have a name that implies otherwise. I don't have a better name. The cat doesn't speak English, though, so I suppose her name doesn't matter.

But I won't call her Ginger.

***

"Cute cat," Stella says, gesturing at the tiny kitten sleeping on my shoulder.

"Thanks, I picked her up yesterday from the shelter."

"Fostering or keeping?" Stella walks around the counter and plucks the feline from my shoulder.

"Keeping. I'm following your advice," I reply, taking a bite of my yogurt.

"I never told you to go get a cat."

"You told me to find someone to love. I love this cat." I take her from Stella and settle her back on my shoulder.

She gives the cat one last scratch before asking, "What's her name?"

"I haven't given her one. Figured I'd call her Cat."

"You can't do that! She needs a name!"

"She doesn't speak English. I'm sure calling her Cat is fine."

"You're going to make me take up smoking again. Give the damn cat a name."

I glance around and spot my empty yogurt container. "Fine. Yogurt. Her name is Yogurt."

"That is *not* a name." She scowls at me.

"It is now."

"I need a cigarette."

***

How does one go about playing with a cat?

I've turned half of my home office into a space for Yogurt, complete with a bed, scratchers, and cat trees. I enjoy watching her while I work. But I would like to have more enjoyment with this tiny ball of fur.

Perhaps if I...

I carefully sit in the middle of the floor near Yogurt as she bats a dangling ball on one of her trees. She might not notice me, but I think I'm enjoying this. Uncertainty almost has me getting up and abandoning all intention of playing, but I remember what Stella said. I should enjoy my life.

So I lie down on the rug.

Even if Yogurt doesn't notice me, I think I am having fun watching the feline from this angle.

The kitten's head snaps in my direction and she jumps off her perch. Yogurt lowers her front half while wiggling her tail before pouncing onto my chest and batting my tie. Something like a laugh breaks free, and I reach up to stroke the soft fur on her head.

I need to get my notebook and log this feeling to examine later, but I don't want the moment to end. Yogurt gave up on my tie and is kneading my chest, purring.

Is this happy?

Eight

Betty

"GIRL, IF YOU REALLY want to piss off your husband, you should bag that guy right over there," Lilith says, leaning over the desk, staring at a handsome man in a tux. He's tall with broad shoulders and rich brown hair. He looks miserable as he makes his way to the bar, every woman's head turning to follow him.

"Who is he?" I ask, mesmerized by his beauty.

"That is Bennett Sterling. *The* Bennett Sterling," she says.

"I don't know who that is."

"Seriously? He owns everything Sterling, like the shopping app? Super rich, super hot. Never seen out and about."

I giggle. "Oh my, that's my husband's boss. He hates him."

"So you should definitely do him and rub it in your husband's face."

"Wouldn't that be something? I can't do it, the whole dating thing. It's enough that my husband thinks I am. You should see his face when I get home in the mornings—looks like his head is going to explode." I cackle.

Lilith chuckles as someone approaches the receptionist's desk, so I wave goodbye and go to the bar. Bennett Sterling is there with a woman hanging off his arm. Poor guy looks so uncomfortable that my heart twinges. I walk close enough to hear what they are saying.

"Why don't we head upstairs to my room?"

"No, thank you," Bennett Sterling says stiffly. The woman leans closer as he tries to pull away from her.

I take a deep breath, gathering my courage. Summoning the woman I used to be, I lay my hand on his shoulder and squeal, "Bennett! I haven't seen you since college! How have you been?"

He looks like a deer caught in headlights, so I tug him into a hug and whisper, "Just play along. I promise I'm not hitting on you."

Feeling him relax slightly, I let him go and turn to the woman. "Hi! I'm Betty, Benny and I go way back. Can I steal him from you so we can catch up? Thanks so much!"

I don't give her a chance to answer before I grab his hand and drag him to an empty booth. He sits down and I gesture for him to scoot over and climb in beside him.

"I figured I would act as a shield between you and that woman, who I might add, is glaring at me."

He releases a puff of air. "Thank you."

"No problem. I love being a hero. But it does look like you are stuck with me for a little bit."

His lip twitches into a small smile. "I don't mind being stuck with you."

"Fantastic! Let's get to know each other. I don't know about you but I could really use a friend."

"I've been told I need a friend, as well."

"Who told you that?" I ask.

"Stella, my housekeeper."

"Is she right?" I'm curious about this handsome man and his housekeeper who thinks he needs a friend.

"My life consists of work, weekly conversations with Stella, and my new cat named Yogurt. She might be right."

"Oh, you have a cat! I love cats!" I chirp, wiggling excitedly in my seat.

"Would you like to see a picture? I have some on my phone," he says, bashfully.

"Yes. I would like that very much."

He directs me to swipe through his photo album and it's the cutest thing I've ever seen. I get to watch this tiny little Siamese kitten grow into a larger kitten and it's magnificent.

"I love your little baby kitty, her name is Yogurt? How'd she get a name like Yogurt?"

"Stella informed me that a cat needs a name. I had intended on calling her Cat, and I was eating a yogurt. Since cats don't speak English, I presume that one name is as good as another."

"I love it. Very practical. Is she a cuddly cat or standoffish?"

"Both. Almost exactly an even split, with her being a touch more cuddly than... what did you call it? Standoffish?" He asks, clearly amused.

"Oh, she sounds like a great little kitten. I always wanted a cat, but my dad is allergic and my husband sucks."

"Husband? You're married?"

"Sadly, yes." I shrug.

"Is your husband going to be upset that you are spending time with me?"

I giggle. "My goodness, I hope so!"

Poor Bennett looks startled and very concerned. "And why is that?"

"Well, it's a dreadful story. But the gist is that my husband asked for an open marriage and now I'm dating myself."

"He sounds terrible."

"He's the worst. I'm so pissed that it took me this long to realize it, you know? I wasted seven years on him and for what? Nothing. He works for you, you know? In the finance department."

Bennett's eyes widen and he tilts his head. "What's his name?"

"Trevor Smith, and his girlfriend is Paige Something-or-other. Why? Gonna fire them for me?" I ask, wiggling my eyebrows dramatically so he knows that I'm joking.

"I wish I could but cannot. I like to place faces with actions."

I really like how straightforward Bennett is.

"Gosh darn it." I laugh. "Maybe you can just give them extra work or something unpleasant."

He pulls out a tiny dark green notebook from his pocket and jots something down.

"Whatcha writing?" I ask, exceedingly curious.

"Making myself a note to do anything that I legally can to make their jobs unpleasant."

"I love having friends in high places!"

"Isn't that a song?"

"Nope," I say, popping the p.

***

"I have actually enjoyed myself tonight. Thank you," Bennett says. The bar is closing down and the waitress strongly suggested that it's time for us to go.

"Me too! Do you want to do this again? Or maybe not this exactly but something together?"

"As friends?" He asks, nervously, hopefully.

Relief washes over me. *Friends.*

"Yes! Why don't we go out for ice cream tomorrow? We can walk from the hotel to the ice cream shop and then the beach. You're staying at the hotel tonight, right?"

A small smile tilts his lips up. "I do have a room for the night. You want to get ice cream and walk on the beach?"

"Yep! Don't you?" I reply, bouncing a little bit in my seat. This is fun.

"I cannot recall ever doing that. But I would love to accompany you."

"It's a friend date, then!"

"A friend date?"

"Yes! A couple friends doing date things. But if we see my husband will you pretend to be my boyfriend?"

"That sounds so bizarre." He gives me a bemused smile. "But yes, I will be your fake boyfriend."

"Oh, goodie!" I giggle and shimmy my shoulders.

"Would you like me to escort you to your room?"

I almost immediately say yes. But I don't actually know this man, even if I feel like we've known each other forever. Maybe I shouldn't let him know which room is mine.

"No, thank you. I'll see you tomorrow!"

***

Bennett

I'm nervously waiting in the lobby of L'albergo Verbania, at exactly 11 a.m.—in the same gray suit I was wearing when I checked in before the gala yesterday. I do wish I had anticipated staying at the hotel and brought an extra set of clothes. It feels wrong to wear the same suit I wore yesterday when I am going on my first friend date. Nothing to be done now. I couldn't very well wear the tux from last night. I stand in front of a pillar near the elevators to wait for Betty. I'm actually excited. I cannot remember the last time I was excited about anything. It seems Stella was right, I do need a friend.

The elevator dings, drawing my attention, and I lock eyes with Betty. She really is a beautiful woman, a little more than half a foot shorter than I am, with amazing curves and bright red hair. Last night, she was in a sexy little black dress, but today, she is dressed like a cotton candy dream. Wearing a baby blue halter romper, pale pink wedge sandals, and a matching bag, she skips toward me, her pink lips smiling brightly.

"Hiya, Benny! I'm so sorry that I'm late. I wish I could say it won't happen again but really it's just who I am as a person." She smiles and I know that I would wait on her as long as she wants me to.

"I never mind waiting."

"Oh, don't tell me that! It will subconsciously make me later, I just know it! Be angry with me so maybe I'll be on time next time."

Without thinking I growl, "Grrr, I'm so angry. Don't be late."

I immediately feel ridiculous, why would I say that? But then she laughs and hugs me and my heart pounds as I wrap my arms around her giving her a little squeeze. She extracts herself from my arms and I feel the loss acutely.

"That was great! You have to growl at me every time I'm late!"

"I will certainly try."

She grabs my hand, dragging me through the hotel lobby and out the door into the bright sunshine. A lightness that I've never felt takes up residence in my chest. Where has this effervescent woman been my whole life?

"Let's go get some ice cream. What's your favorite flavor?" she asks, bouncing down the sidewalk, her little hand tucked into mine—pulling me along with her on this adventure.

"I don't really know. Chocolate, perhaps? I cannot remember the last time that I had ice cream."

"That's terrible! They do samples here so we can try a few flavors and find your favorite!"

"Sounds like a plan. What's your favorite?" I ask, excited to add another like to her list in my pocket notebook.

"Cotton candy with pink sprinkles! And if they don't have cotton candy I get the cheesecake flavor."

I barely restrain myself from grabbing my little notebook and jotting down her preferences. I'll do it later.

I never noticed the charm of this town. I could see someone as vibrant as Betty living here. The shops are all brightly colored, and Verbania Sweets and Treats is ahead. It's bright teal with a canary yellow door. An assortment of candies decorate the windows. I pull open the door for Betty, and she grins at me as she walks inside. This sugar-filled wonderland is instantly overwhelming, and I hate it. I make a mental note to never invite Betty to this particular shop again. If she wants ice cream, we'll go somewhere else.

Betty turns and spins her arms out with a bright "Ta-da!" But whatever she sees on my face has her looking worried.

"Oh, no. You hate it," she says, a cute pout on her face.

"I don't hate it," I say, then correct myself. "Okay. I do hate it. It is so crowded and cluttered that it feels like I can't breathe in here."

That was way too much information. Why would I tell her that? I could have said that I didn't hate it.

This is why I don't bother with friends. Last time I even tried was in grade school and hearing my supposed friend tell me that "no one cares," crushed my want for companionship.

But then she giggles and takes my hand. "Don't worry, the ice cream here will more than make it up to you!"

"We'll see," I utter warily, making her laugh.

She looks at me as if to check if I am actually okay, and then drags me to the ice cream counter. I am quickly flustered by the sheer amount of ice cream available. She squeezes my hand and says, "They do a sample tray here, we can get a couple bites of each flavor and try them all. Figure out which flavor is your favorite and all that jazz!"

Relieved that I don't have to decide and I get to take my time I smile at her gratefully. "Yes, let's do that."

A few minutes later, we are all set up with what looks like a huge egg carton of ice cream flavors and two spoons. She leads me to their outdoor seating, and I instantly breathe a sigh of relief.

"It's really nice out here," I say, taking in the teal and yellow tables and the view of the park across the road.

"It is. This whole town is one of my favorite places. And a lot of the shops are women owned, which is really cool." She bounces in her seat, excited to tell me about this city.

"I didn't know that. I am not very familiar with this area. I spend most of my time in Coslada working."

"Lame! Looks like I'm going to have to work extra hard to get you to have fun," she chirps, studying the ice cream situation.

"I think I would enjoy that."

She gives me a blinding smile that makes my heart skip a beat. She really is pretty, and says, "Okay, you should start with cotton candy because it is the best flavor. And then we can end with chocolate because you know you like that one. I always like to end on a positive note."

"Good plan," I say, taking the spoon from her outstretched hand. Then I take out my pocket notebook and open it to a clean page.

"What's with the notebook?" Betty asks.

"Well, I figure we can make notes on what flavors we like. Could be interesting to see our favorites and least favorites. Plus we can determine the best flavor at this shop," I reply, feeling preposterous. Taunts of schoolboys swirl through my head, making it hard to breathe.

"Oh my goodness! I love that! A science experiment with ice cream!"

The tightness in my chest unravels at her praise. I don't have to be on guard with my words, she seems to enjoy what I have to say. I've never had that before.

The next hour passes in a blur as we taste and rate ice cream flavors deciding that cotton candy is the very best, even though I prefer pistachio above all others, and that salted caramel is the worst. I had no idea that I had strong opinions on salted caramel, but caramel is way better without the salt.

"This is fantastic! Next time we come here you don't even have to go inside since we know your favorites!" Betty chatters as we clean up the table and dispose of our trash.

"That would be ideal."

"I'm sorry that you hated it," she says, placing the tray on top of the trash can.

"I enjoyed eating ice cream with you," I reply, hoping that she isn't upset I don't like the chaotic shop.

"I'm having fun, too! Let's walk down to the beach." Betty grabs my hand leading me off the patio and onto the sidewalk. She doesn't let go of my hand and I like that.

It's about a 20-minute stroll to the beach from the center of town but it feels like seconds with Betty holding my hand.

Verbania Beach isn't crowded, all white sand and glimmering water.

"Let's go put our feet in the sea!" Betty squeals, grabbing my arm to stabilize her as she removes her sandals.

"I'm not dressed for swimming," I reply.

She giggles and says, "That's okay. Leave the shoes and roll up your pants. We're just going to get our little piggies wet."

I pull off my socks and shoes and then roll up my pant legs awkwardly.

"I look ridiculous," I mutter before I can stop myself.

Immediately, she smiles and looks me up and down.

"I think you look hot."

She says it so casually that I can't help but believe her.

***

Betty

I can't believe I told him that he looks hot! Who says that to a very new friend? Me apparently. At least he looks pleased. It would have sucked if he took it in a less-than-platonic kind of way.

I grab his hand and drag him across the sand not stopping until our feet are in the water.

"It's cold."

I bark out a laugh, goosebumps racing up my legs. "Sure is!"

"It is rather unpleasant," he complains.

"That's why we only put our feet in."

"Why should we put in any body part?" he asks, tugging my shivering self out of the water and back onto the warm sand.

"Because it's fun. Aren't you having fun?"

"I, uh, yes. Actually, yes," he stammers, looking surprised.

I shimmy my shoulders and wiggle my hips in excitement. "Let's go over there and watch the water!"

"We didn't bring chairs or a blanket."

"That's alright, we can just sit in the sand. Unless that'll ruin your pants or something,"

"No, no. My clothes will be fine. We can sit in the sand," Bennett replies, looking like he would prefer to chew off his own hand.

But I pretend not to notice and drag him down. Pulling my legs under me, I run my fingers through the shimmery white sand. Bennett is comically grimacing as he tries to make himself comfortable in the sand without actually touching the sand.

"So, do you like being the big boss man? Or is it something you just fell into?" I ask, wanting to figure out what makes this uptight man tick.

He looks thoughtful before replying, "I don't usually think of my life in terms of like or dislike. I have responsibilities and that is a fact of my life. But to answer your question, yes, I do believe that I enjoy my work. However, it was what I was raised for. I've never considered doing anything else."

"Never? Not even when you were little? You didn't want to be a wrestler or a firefighter-superhero or something?"

I see a little smile try to break free on his handsome face as he replies, "I've always known that I would be CEO and primary owner of the Sterling Corporation. There was no other option."

"I guess your parents weren't big on imagination and pretend play, huh?"

"Absolutely not."

I pluck a tiny shell from the sand, running my thumb over the tiny indents, and bump him with my shoulder.

"Maybe our next friend date should be a cosplay convention or something, then we can both pretend!"

***

Bennett

"Lookie who's doing the walk of shame at 4 p.m. on a Sunday wearing the same suit he left the house in." Stella laughs as she folds my laundry on the kitchen table.

My cheeks heat as I scramble for a reply.

"I didn't intend to stay the night."

"Oh, hell yeah! Let me grab you a cup of coffee and then you're telling me everything," Stella says excitedly, stomping over to the coffee maker.

"That isn't necessary."

"Sure, it is. This is what friends do. They talk about exciting things that happen in their lives. And you meeting a girl is very exciting."

"I didn't meet a girl, I mean, I did but not in a romantic way. We're just going to be friends."

"That's just as good, sugar. You need friends. Now, tell me all about it."

Stella brings me a cup of coffee fixed exactly as I like it—black. I wonder how Betty takes her coffee, probably like Stella with lots of cream and sugar. Thinking of Betty's likes and dislikes, I pull out my pocket notebook and start a list of her likes: a lemon drop cocktail, cotton candy ice cream, Verbania, the beach, and retro clothes. I scowl at the list, disappointed that I don't know more about her. Stella is grinning at me when I look up, and I have the barely containable urge to run away.

"I don't know what you want me to say," I mumble.

Another laugh. "Alright, let's start at the beginning. How did you meet her?"

"I went to the bar after my speech and she saved me from a very flirty woman."

"Hell yeah, boy! Tell me more about this flirty woman!"

"She kept trying to get me to go up to her hotel room. I didn't like it. I told her 'no thanks' but she wouldn't leave me alone." I say, exasperated.

"You sweet baby angel. I bet you did say 'no, thank you' didn't you?"

"Of course I did. I pride myself on being polite."

Stella chuckles and shakes her head. "I know you do, baby angel. Now, how did this new friend of yours save you?"

"She walked right up to me and acted like she was an old friend. And grabbed my arm and practically dragged me away. We then talked until the bar closed, about four hours."

Yogurt bounds into the kitchen, meowing for me to pick her up. I do so and place her on my shoulder.

"You talked for four hours?"

"Yes."

"Well?" She asks, rotating her hand.

"Her name is Betty."

"Thanks, that tells me a lot." She huffs.

Nine

Bennett

"Stella only comes on Wednesdays and Sundays, so you won't get to meet her today," I say, unlocking my dark-wood front door.

"Well, then I'll have to come over on a weekend so I can meet the infamous Stella."

I like the sound of that—a lot.

"You will love Stella."

She giggles. "I'm sure I will."

I look around my small home, wondering how it looks to a woman as vivacious as Betty. I gave my credit card to Stella and told her to keep it uncluttered, and she did an excellent job creating a home that I am comfortable in.

The walls are a cream color with minimal wall decor and a few abstract pieces—deep reds and greens with some yellow and black slashed through. All dark wood and brown leather furniture, with absolutely no dust collectors. The only items on display in my house are books, mostly my vintage encyclopedia sets. Stella decorated the whole house the same way, even the kitchen and bathrooms.

"I love it!" she says, clapping her hands and looking around.

"You do?" I ask, quite surprised at her exuberance over my minimalist home.

"Of course I do! I just knew your home would suit you so perfectly!"

"Stella decorated it." I don't want her to think that I have any inclination toward home decorating.

"She knows you so well, then. I can so see you being all at home here, which is good since it is your home."

I chuckle. "Yes, I suppose it is."

A little jingle bouncing down the hall interrupts us. Yogurt, the little bell on her collar tinkling, hops into the living room, startles, and runs under the sofa.

Betty squeals, and I smile at her. "Well, that was Yogurt. I am sure she will come out in a couple of minutes."

"Oh. My. Goodness! I cannot wait to cuddle that little baby kitty!"

"Could I get you a water while we wait?" I ask, wanting to make Betty comfortable in my home.

"Oh, yes, please!" She watches the couch as if she might miss the cat if she looks away.

In the kitchen, I grab two glasses and fill them from the pitcher in the refrigerator. I take a moment to gather myself. I've never had a visitor in my home. This is strange but good, especially since my visitor is Betty.

A squeak and the tinkling of a bell draw me back into the living room. Betty, her hair held off her face with a wide baby blue headband and wearing a '60s wide-leg pink jumpsuit, is sitting cross-legged on my floor, Yogurt in her lap.

I pull out my phone and snap a photo, the first one I have ever taken of another person, and sit next to Betty.

"Can I make this my phone background?" I ask, showing Betty the picture.

"Oh my goodness!" she chirps, bouncing and clutching the cat. "You want me and Yogurt as your background? Yes! Of course! Oh, can we take a selfie to be mine?"

"You want a picture of us?"

"Of course, now scootch in," she demands, holding her phone up, getting all three of us in the frame. Her cotton candy scent wraps around me as she snaps the picture and shows me. It's the best photo I have ever seen. Betty is mid-laugh, holding Yogurt and glorious.

"Please send that to me. I want to make it my lock screen."

"Really? I get your lock screen and background! We really are best friends, Benny-Boo!"

Happiness radiates through me, even as a small knot of worry forms in my chest. Can I do this whole best friend thing? I've never had a best friend before.

"Look! We are so freaking cute!" Betty giggles, shoving her phone in my face. I smile, certain my cheeks will be sore at the end of the day, and I show her my phone.

***

Betty

"And what exactly is needle felting?" Bennett asks, shutting the car door and starting the engine.

Trying to keep Bennett all to myself—and away from Trevor—I always meet Bennett at his house or the date spot. Yes, I want Trevor to be jealous, thinking I'm out on dates but I don't want to cause any problems for Bennett at work. Or have Trevor wreck this.

"You know felt, the material? Well, it's made by taking wool and punching it with a needle over and over. Doesn't really sound like a lot of fun, but the results are super cool," I say. "Hang on, I grabbed the brochure—somewhere in here..." I add, rummaging through my purse until I find it.

"We're making fabric? Or are we turning the fabric into something?"

"We're making Halloween ornaments. Whatever that means. Oh, like for a Halloween tree! You should get a Halloween tree!"

His lips tilt up in a small smile. "Only if you decorate it."

"Seriously? I would love to!"

"Set up a wish list on the Sterling app and fill it with a Halloween tree and everything else needed to decorate it. Send it to me and I will have it ready for you by next week."

"Wait. Seriously? You're going to put up a tree in your house for me to decorate?" I bounce in my seat.

"Of course. We will need a place to display our felted ornaments and this is a marvelous solution."

"Yes, it's perfect!"

***

Bennett

Pumpkin ornaments packed in a tiny bag, Betty drags me out of Felting Flora, all giggles and sunshine.

"Want to have lunch with me? We could try the bistro across the park." Betty says, bouncing on the balls of her feet.

"I would love to," I reply, elated to get more time with Betty.

It is so difficult to believe that she enjoys spending time with me. I've had people over the years try to befriend me for money or connections, but Betty only asks for my company. She even tried to pay for our class today. Which was kind of her, but unnecessary. At this point, I believe I would pay Betty for her companionship. Actually, I know I would—all she would have to do is ask.

I never truly understood the concept of friends until Betty. Two people decide to spend time together regularly? But with Betty, every day I spend with her, the more crucial to my life she becomes.

"Betty!" a feminine voice calls from across the park.

She drops my hand, yelling, "Lilith!"

I feel the loss keenly. An emptiness creeps into my chest as I watch Betty and the pink-haired woman embrace and chatter. I consider polite ways to excuse myself, not wanting Betty to feel obligated to our lunch plans.

But then Betty is grabbing my hand again, tugging me into their conversation.

"Bennett, this is Lilith. Lilith, meet Bennett. There! Now we're all friends!" she chirps happily.

"Nice to meet you, Lilith." I extend my hand—the hand that Betty is not holding—to shake Lilith's.

"So formal! I love it! What are you guys up to?" Lilith asks, grinning.

"Grabbing lunch right now, we took a class at Felting Flora."

"Oh, I'm starving. Can I come with?" Lilith asks, wiggling her eyebrows.

Betty giggles and looks to me, eyes dancing with the silent question.

"Of course," I reply.

I'm uneasy, still considering excusing myself.

But Betty squeezes my hand, smiles at me, and I don't want to go. I'm surprised that I actually *want* to have lunch with Betty *and* Lilith. And even more surprising, I think they want to spend time with me, too.

I'm proven right when Lilith squeaks and takes my other hand. The women drag me through the park, a steady stream of chatter surrounding me.

"Oh! We should do a group costume and set up at the trunk-or-treat! It's next weekend! Mira is always looking for more people to hand out candy!" Lilith rambles. "I don't really know what we could be, maybe superheroes or something!"

"Oh my god. That sounds like so much fun! What do you think?" Betty says, looking at me.

It sounds terrible.

"What is a trunk-or-treat?" I ask, hoping it is a nice quiet affair. But knowing that it is not.

"It's so much fun! So technically, you're supposed to decorate the trunk of your car and fill it with candy for the kids to trick-or-treat. But this one everyone sets up little booths, all themed out. I've always wanted to do one but didn't want to do it alone." Lilith sighs. "No one ever wants to trunk-or-treat with me."

"We do! Don't we, Benny-Boo?"

We.

Benny-Boo.

Betty smiling up at me.

Before I can come up with an excuse, I find myself saying, "I would love to."

Both ladies shriek and hug me. I freeze, my heart pounding. Being friends with Betty is one thing. It feels—not natural, but like it's meant to be. Lilith, though. I was nervous about one friendship with a vibrant woman, but two? What am I even doing here? Surely, they would have more fun without me.

Maybe they're just being nice.

"You can be Batman! Wouldn't he be the perfect Batman?" Betty says, patting my arm.

"Yes! Oh, yes! That gives us a lot of options for our costumes, too!"

We arrive at Butler's Bistro, and I pull the door open for the twittering ladies. They have decided that they need my measurements and will pick up our costumes the day of the event. And then get dressed at my house.

Both of them in my home.

My hand itches to pull out my notebook. I need to write all this down to think about later. Instead I'm pulled to a table, and a menu is shoved into my hand.

The women chatter, pulling me into the conversation. Betty jokes about how I get the same thing everywhere, Lilith agreeing with me. Our food comes as I relax, enjoying myself immensely.

A steady stream of conversation flows around me, involving me but not pressuring me, lively and fun.

Even though I am mostly silent, Betty and Lilith are still planning, still laughing—and I... well, I'm laughing, too.

Ten

Bennett

Leaning against the counter, I cannot help but smile at Betty as she twirls around my kitchen. She's making sugar cookies, or as she said, "fake sugar cookies." I've never had one and she demanded that we immediately buy the supplies and go to my house to make them. So, of course, I obliged.

I had to take a work call, and I don't think she realizes I'm back.

Betty is singing to herself—very off-key—narrating what she is doing.

"Two eggs, one two eggs, crack 'em, crack 'em eggs. Ooh de lally, golly, two eggs," she sings, slightly shaking her hips.

A laugh sneaks out of me, startling both of us. I only seem to laugh around her.

Betty spins around, hand on her heart, her cheeks flushed. "Oh goodness, you startled me."

"I'm sorry, but I really do like your little song," I say, smiling at her red face.

"I don't even realize I'm doing it." She covers her face with her hands and giggles.

I pull her hands down and duck my head to look into her downturned face. "I think it's cute."

She lightly slaps my chest. "Silly goose, get back in your pond."

"Honk, honk," I reply, both of us laughing.

We jump when Stella, chuckling, says, "Whatcha cooking?"

"Betty is making me sugar cookies." I know my face matches Betty's flush.

"Sugar cookies, huh? Is that what the kids are calling it these days?"

"Well, yes, I would assume that children also call them sugar cookies," I reply, looking at Betty for confirmation.

"Yep! Or maybe those soft-cookies-with-the-icing?" Betty agrees with a chuckle.

Stella looks at us and then bursts into laughter. I'm confused—Betty's joke was funny, but I don't believe it was *that* funny.

"Oh, my sweet angel baby, it looks like you found another sweet angel baby to go and do sweet angel baby things with. I am going to love hearing all about it," Stella says, patting me on the cheek and leaving the kitchen.

Betty tilts her head to the side, giggling. "Sweet angel baby?"

"It's one of her many terms of endearment."

"Oh, I love that! I think I might steal it. Now, let me get these cookies in the oven before they melt."

She scurries away, bringing light into my life where there was only monotony. I'm having fun, something I've never had before. Even in childhood, I was a serious little thing, and any whimsy was quickly squashed under my father's heel. He isn't a cruel man, just stern with high expectations. Luckily for both of us, I met those high expectations. Now I get sugar cookies and Halloween trees.

Betty claps. "Alright, we have about eight minutes until they're done."

"Why don't you two sit down and let me make a pot of coffee. Then we can talk, Betty," Stella says as she briskly walks into the kitchen, shooing us over to the table.

"Sounds like we're in trouble," Betty whispers, making me chuckle.

"I heard that!" Stella snarks, making Betty blush again.

Yogurt saunters into the kitchen, moving between Stella's legs, causing her to trip and snap, "You damn cat, get out from under me!"

Betty leans down, clicking her tongue. "Come here, Yogurt."

Yogurt, noticing Betty, skips over to her and meows loudly. Another smile erupts on my face as Betty squeaks and picks her up, cuddling their cute faces together. Sudden jealousy makes my chest feel tight, but I don't know which one I'm jealous of. I think I want to be a part of their cuddles. I quickly excuse myself, rushing into my bedroom.

Pulling out my pocket notebook, I write a quick note to myself. *Jealousy, Betty and Yogurt. Do I want affection?*

Something to untangle later. Now's not the time.

I splash cold water on my face, letting the sensation shock the knotted feeling from my stomach.

Anxious to get back, I hurry down the hall to find Stella, sitting next to Betty, both of them laughing.

Stella looks at me with an eyebrow raised. "You'll never guess how Betty takes her coffee."

I glance at Betty's baffled expression and try to think of a funny coffee order but I don't think there is one. "You're right. I will never guess."

"Black, just like you!" She laughs again.

I like that Betty and I have the same taste in coffee, but I am unsure why that's funny. At least I don't have to rush to write this preference in my notebook as I'm very unlikely to forget it.

"Twinsies!" Betty exclaims, making me smile.

Stella looks back and forth between us before grinning and saying, "Sweet baby angels. I'll get out of y'all's hair, have fun!"

"Thank you for the coffee! I'm glad that I got to meet you!" Betty chirps, giving Stella a tiny wave.

"Right back at ya, chicky. I'll see you Wednesday, Bennett." Stella stomps out of the kitchen to gather her things.

Betty and I sit in silence, her nuzzling Yogurt and me trying not to stare. The front door clicks as Stella leaves, slamming the door behind her.

"Bennett. She's wonderful!" Betty says, patting my hand. The oven timer dings and Betty drops the cat on the floor before checking on her cookies.

"Where's an oven mitt?" she asks, looking over her shoulder at me.

The bite of unease barrels into me. "I actually don't know. Stella is the only one who cooks in here."

Betty grins and starts opening drawers and cabinets, finding them quickly. She pulls out the cookies and sets the baking sheet on the stovetop. I move beside her to admire her creation, soft cookies with orange and black Halloween sprinkles.

"They look delicious," I say.

"Thank you! We still have to wait for them to cool, though." She sighs, looking at the cookies.

"Why don't we get your Halloween tree set up while we wait?"

Betty squeals and pokes my arm. "I cannot believe you got me a tree to decorate!"

"I did tell you that I would."

"You sure did! Let's go!" She giggles, pushing me out of the vanilla scented kitchen.

I settle her in the living room while I retrieve what looks like half of the Halloween section on the Sterling App. Her laughter bounces off the walls as I carry the little tree out, and note that I've never looked forward to decorating anything until now.

The tree she picked out is a spooky, leafless thing intended for a tabletop. I set it up on the coffee table, looking forward to seeing it every day. Betty starts to sort out the decorations, opening boxes and finding hooks for the orange and black ornaments.

"We should save our felted ornaments for last, so we can give them the best spot!"

I agree and we start hanging the eerie items. Betty is chaotic in her placement, twirling around the tree while I take longer to decide on a spot. In a moment Betty has finished her stash and claps her hands while I carefully hang mine in the holes.

"We make the best team!" She chirps, picking up our handmade trinkets and handing me the one she made.

My face is hot, my mouth is dry, and Betty wants me to choose the spot for her ornament. I study the tree and choose a branch at the top, where it's easiest to see. Betty hugs me suddenly, and before I can react she's gone, placing my felted pumpkin on the branch next to hers.

"Now they're best friends!"

***

I look ridiculous.

There isn't a mirror in my home office, so I'm using the camera on my phone. I pull the collar away from my clammy skin, heat traveling up my neck to my ears.

I can't go out there like this.

"Batman! Batman! Batman!" Betty and Lilith chant from the other side of the door.

The ladies showed up with costumes and makeup bags, chattering and hugging me. They took over my bedroom almost two hours ago, refusing to let me see them during that time. It was nice to hear giggles bouncing through my apartment as I worked and watched Yogurt.

Twenty minutes ago they yelled for me to go put on the costume that Betty bought me. I regret agreeing to this excursion.

I flap my hands, trying to shake these nerves away, and open the door.

Every coherent thought vanishes the moment I see Betty. She's radiant—cleavage framed in a skintight green jumpsuit, wild hair cascading around her face, her makeup vivid. Heart pounding, I search for anything to say.

Betty and Lilith both compliment me on being the perfect Batman while I gather my bearings.

"Thank you, ladies. You both look lovely. What are the names of your characters?" I ask once I've caught my breath.

Lilith grins and adjusts her cat ears. "I'm Catwoman and Betty is Poison Ivy. We're all from the same comic book."

I should have researched.

"Don't worry!" Betty chirps. "Batman is a man of few words, so you can let me and Lils do all the talking!"

"So I am to stand there and put candy in children's buckets?" I want to be prepared for tonight.

"Yup!" Lilith exclaims, grabbing my hand and tugging me down the hall, Betty bouncing behind me.

***

Betty

The trunk-or-treat is in full swing and poor Bennett is sweating bullets. Amid the laughter and music, he's standing behind our comic-book-themed table handing out candy and little toys to the swarming children.

But he looks miserable.

I walk around to stand next to him. "I'm sorry I dragged you into this."

He jolts, turning to me with wide eyes. "Why are you sorry?"

"I know you're uncomfortable, I should've realized—"

"No, I'm actually enjoying myself," he interrupts. "I *am* uncomfortable but this is good."

"Are you sure? Because we can leave early if you want or maybe you could change or something," I say, fidgeting with a leaf on my sleeve.

"I'm absolutely sure. I really do enjoy interacting with the children."

"Okay, good. Just, you know, let me know if it's too much or whatever."

Relieved, I wrap my arms around him without a second thought. He stiffens, like he always does when I surprise hug him, then he wraps his arms around me.

This feels like home.

Lilith bounces over, throwing her arms around the both of us, smooshing her face into my hair.

"Group hug!" She exclaims, before we all unravel from one another.

Laughing, I look up at Bennett to find him staring at me with a bemused smile on his face. Butterflies erupt in my stomach as our eyes meet and I look down, stepping away to deal with the princesses and pirates wreaking havoc on our table.

***

I toss my Poison Ivy costume over the back of the rocking chair in my bedroom—the guest room that I've been using as a bedroom, that is.

This sterile white-walled room with its generic beige art and white bedspread. I hate it. The only color is my clothes in the closet and my cosmetics on the vanity. The hot pinks and baby blues look startling against the basic palette.

I flick the lock on the bedroom door when I hear our front door chime, alerting me to Trevor getting home. I try to avoid him when we happen to be in the house together, usually staying in my new room.

It's exhausting being a prisoner in my own home.

Footsteps go up the stairs, down the hall, pausing in front of my door.

Keep going, motherfucker.

A gentle tap on the door.

"Bethy?" Trevor asks, his voice sweet in a way I haven't heard in years.

I should have hit the lights and pretended to be asleep.

"Bethany, please, baby. Talk to me," he slurs out.

Great, he's been drinking. Tonight is going to be fun.

"Just go to bed," I say, proud of the acid in my tone.

I hear a thump against the door as Trevor slides down, sitting on the other side.

"I just, I just miss you so much."

"Go to bed, Trevor. We'll talk when you're sober."

Or never.

"I know I fucked up. I know it, but Bethy, you aren't giving me the chance to make it right. You have to forgive me, you're *my* wife! My wife!"

"Not any more. Not since you decided that you wanted an open marriage," I say sadly.

Trevor sobs. "Please, don't say that. Please. I'll change, I, uh, I'll dump Paige. I'll do anything."

I want to feel victorious—I want to revel in his misery. But I can't. I'm just sad.

Trevor is pathetic and my little revenge isn't even fun.

"Please, just leave me alone. Go to bed."

"No! Please Bethy, it didn't mean anything. It's just sex, please. Don't you miss me? Bethy, I miss you so much."

I want to climb out of the window.

"Damn it, Trevor! No! I don't fucking miss you! Go away!"

His sobbing only becomes louder at my harsh words. My heart aches, and I want to console him. But I also want to kick him in the knee caps.

But mostly, I want to be done.
Done with this. Done with him.
I want to be free.

Eleven

Betty

APPLYING BRIGHT PINK LIPSTICK, I wait for Bennett to answer the phone.

"Hello, Betty. How are you doing this morning?"

"I'm so good. What are you up to?" I chirp, blotting my lips.

"I'm having yogurt with Yogurt."

I laugh and say, "Send me a selfie! I want to see!"

"As you wish."

There's a light rustling, then my phone dings with a message. I click it open and shriek—it's Bennett looking so handsome in a gray athletic shirt with Yogurt sitting on his broad shoulder.

"Benny-Boo! I love this! I'm going to set it as the picture that pops up when you call!"

"I'm glad that you like it."

"Oh, I do. So, want to go apartment hunting? I've decided that it's time to get my own place."

"I would be delighted to accompany you. Would you like me to have my realtor pull some listings?"

"Nope, I'm moving to Verbania. There are only a few places for rent, and I have the keys waiting for me at the Wilmslow Museum—that's where the only realtor in town works. I probably should have mentioned that before you agreed. Still want to come with?"

I finish wrapping my hair up in a scarf. I'm going casual today with a pale pink boat-neck top and baby blue pedal pushers.

"Yes, would you like me to drive?"

"Oh yes! You wouldn't mind?" I ask, pulling on my ruffled socks.

"Of course not. When would you like to go?"

"I'm ready now! Whenever you want to go works for me. We can even grab lunch and maybe go to the beach or something. Make a day of it, if you aren't too busy!"

"I would love to make a day of it. Give me about 30 minutes and I will be there to pick you up."

"Perfect. See you soon!"

***

"I want to go back and look around!" I say, patting Bennett's arm. I glance over my shoulder, Wilmslow Museum of Modern Art behind us.

"Would you like to do that today, or shall we plan another outing?"

"Let's plan another date, I don't want to overload today."

"Sounds great. I will make a note of it. Perhaps we can tour all the museums."

"No perhaps! Let's do it, and we can try a new restaurant after each visit! What fun!" I reply, tugging his arm.

I'm so excited I can barely contain myself. Lucky for me, Bennett was able to come with me today. I can really use his steady head since all I want to do is squeal and touch things. We decided to walk to the rentals—it's such a lovely day. Feels like Verbania is nothing but sunshine and I love it.

"Okay, this is the first one," I say, checking the sheet of paper with the rental information on it.

It's a regular-looking house. Light bricks, a dark green door, and matching shutters. I don't love it but do I need to love my first rental after leaving my husband? Any place is better than the home I share with him.

Bennett is looking at me thoughtfully. "Do you want to see the inside, or have you already made your mind up?"

"Oh, I definitely need to look inside. It doesn't have to be perfect, right?" I ask, disappointed.

"No, I suppose it doesn't. But you are already displeased and we haven't even made it onto the front porch. You shouldn't have to settle for a house simply because it is available."

You shouldn't have to settle.

I let those words wrap around my heart. All I've done is settle. I settled for comfort over passion. I settled for a wedding I didn't want. I settled for a husband who didn't treat me as I deserved. I settled in a house that I didn't love.

I smile up at Bennett, so happy that he's my friend. His blunt but kind way of phrasing stuff is one of my favorite things about him.

He gives me a little smile back that makes my heart skip a beat.

"You're so right. I don't have to settle, do I? I can have what I want, can't I?"

"Correct. If you don't find a house you love, perhaps I can purchase a house that you love and you can rent from me. Or I could give it to you, if you would accept."

"I can't let you buy me a house!" I laugh.

"You could. But I assumed you wouldn't. Either way, the offer stands."

"What a way to ruin our friendship! What if I'm a horrible tenant and never pay rent on time and trash whatever lovely house you buy?"

"You wouldn't. But even if you did, I wouldn't want to accept rent from you, regardless. And I can easily afford to hire people to clean whatever mess you create," he says, looking very serious.

"Being friends with a gazillionaire is wild," I shake my head and lead Bennett down the sidewalk to the next rental.

This one is a total improvement over the last. White board-and-batten siding with yellow shutters and a light wood door. It even has flower boxes on the windows full of bright geraniums.

I pull out the correct set of keys and let us inside—to utter disappointment. This house is the opposite of open concept with the front door leading straight into a dark living room with tiny windows. The kitchen is through a narrow entryway and is equally as dark. The house has three bedrooms, which I already thought was too much space for just me, but combined with the closed off living spaces—I hate it.

"Well, this one isn't it," I whine, taking Bennett's hand and dragging him out of that cave.

We look at three other places. The last one is pretty alright—bright and airy—but the exterior is baby poop green.

"Why would anyone paint their house this color?"

"I cannot imagine. It is rather horrible, isn't it?" He retorts, helping me down the stairs.

"But I do love the inside. Two bedrooms is a bit much for just me, but I can always set up a writing room—that would be super cool."

"Except the unfortunate exterior color."

"Yes, *except* for that." I sigh, frustration racing through my veins.

"Let me take you out for a treat. Perhaps we can visit the ice cream shop? Then afterwards we can have an early dinner?"

"Yes, please! I really need some ice cream right now."

"I know you do."

***

We stop by the museum to return the rental keys, and the lovely realtor promises to call me as soon as anything else opens up. She's expecting a loft to be available in a few weeks, so that gives me hope.

"I think a loft would be perfect for me," I say, pulling Bennett towards Verbania Sweets and Treats.

"I agree. You were quite displeased with too much space."

"I really was. It's just me, my books, and some thrift store treasures. I *really* hope this loft is cute. But like, it has to be, right? With a name like Dandelion Haven? Can't have ugly houses in a cutely named neighborhood."

"I believe I've heard that somewhere," Bennett replies before grimacing at the brightly colored shop we've arrived at.

"You go have a seat and I'll get our ice creams. You want pistachio, right?" I can't resist laughing at the relief in his face. He does not like this place.

"Thank you, that will be lovely," he says, handing me his card.

"Absolutely not! This is my treat, to thank you for coming with me today."

"I insist. I always enjoy my time with you, and nothing would please me more than to treat you."

"Well, since you insisted." I giggle, taking his card.

Twelve

Betty

"Would you allow me to get my car and take you to yours? I don't want you to get wet," Bennett says upon realizing that it's raining.

After having the most delicious lunch imaginable, we're leaving Butler's Bistro, a cute and snazzy French restaurant in Verbania. Unbeknownst to us, a heavy rain started while we were laughing, and now we have about half a mile to walk back to our cars.

"Ever the gentleman." I smile up at him. "No, let's just run through it."

"Are you sure? I really don't mind going on my own. Your dress is too lovely to ruin."

His face turns bright red as he delivers the compliment.

"Oh, it'll be fun! And I'm not worried about this dress, it can handle a little rain!" I chirp, grabbing his hand and pulling him out the door.

Like wading into a warm pool, I giggle as I drag him down the sidewalk. By the time we reach the fountain, we're drenched.

Bennett wears a bemused expression as I stop and demand that he dance with me.

"Right here? In the rain?"

"Of course!" I reply, taking his hand and moving into his arms. I hum a song that I don't know the lyrics to and sway to the sound. He lets me lead, but tightens his arms around me a little bit. Rain pours down my face, taking my mascara with it, and all I can see is Bennett's little smile.

The rain stops as suddenly as it started—the sun emerges from behind the clouds and I'm in Bennett's arms. We lean into each other, lost in the sunshine, until a group of children run around us, startling us apart.

I laugh as three harried mothers follow behind them, giving us a look of apology but keeping their focus on the children.

"That was so much fun!" I exclaim, putting my hand on Bennett's chest. He looks down at me, amusement dancing in his eyes, his cheeks flushed.

"It was. I have never done anything enjoyable during a storm."

"Same! We will have to have more dates in the rain!"

"I'll be sure to check the forecast before our next outing," he says, leading me to our cars.

***

"Loft, loft, loft. I got a loft. A cute little loft in Dan, Dan, Dandelion Haven, ven, ven," I sing to myself, alone in the tiny breakroom at work. I just got off the phone with the realtor. She has the cutest little loft available. Jen was kind enough to send me pictures since I'm at work and can't go check it out in person. I'm in love. It's tiny and light and airy and perfect. I'm going to meet her there to sign the paperwork, as long as it's as magnificent as the pictures.

"Gotta get a snack, snack, snack, so I can go back to work, work, work. Do dee do daa." I continue my little song, shaking my hips as I grab a granola bar.

"Nice song." Fable laughs, walking into the little room. "We should make it our company bop."

My face heats. I can't believe my boss caught me singing and dancing.

I have to quit now.

"Oh my god. I, uh—I was excited." I shove the granola bar into my mouth.

Clearly amused, Fable grabs a coffee cup and asks, "Good news?"

"Very! I'm pretty sure I found a rental here! A little loft, it looks perfect from the pictures!"

"Oh, those over on Dandelion? I could see you living there, very cute."

I squeal. "I sure hope so! I'm dying to get out of Coslada."

"I can imagine. I could never live in a big city like that."

"Yeah, it's not for everyone. I like it—but I love it here."

Meredith pokes her head in. "Hey, the store's filling up. We'll all need to be out there in a few minutes."

"Yes, ma'am," Fable says, chugging down his coffee.

I have my mouth full of granola so I wave in acknowledgment.

The rest of the day flies by. There is a live band and some food trucks in the park, so we ended up with a ton of business. I had planned on asking Bennett to meet me after work to tour the apartment but I forgot to text him. *Damn it.*

I check my phone for the address and drive the three minutes to find my—hopefully—new house.

I pull into the driveway and know: I'm home.

***

"Alright, little lady, I think that's the last box. Ready to hit the road?" Dad asks.

"Yep. You and Mom go ahead. Danny, will you ride with me?"

"Sure will," Danny replies.

My parents leave and Danny turns to me, smirking. "Alright, what are we up to?"

I laugh. "Well, I bought some shrimp that would fit nicely in the curtain rods and some salmon for the air vents. Oh! And I found this Sneaky-Stinky spray that I'm going to pour into his cologne."

"Sneaky-Stinky?"

"Yeah, it's supposed to smell good for the first hour or so, then over time it starts to smell increasingly terrible. So he won't even know that he stinks unless someone tells him!" I say, dancing around in excitement.

"Oh, that's brutal. I love it. It's a lot less than the twerp deserves, though. Let's take all the batteries in the house, too!"

"Yes! And all the labels off of the canned food!" I whoop, so glad that my brother could come help today.

"Devious! How long do we have until the twerp gets home?"

"Well, he should be served with divorce papers in about an hour at his mom's house. I figure he'll come this way when he gets them."

Danny claps his hands. "Looks like we don't have a lot of time to fuck shit up so let's get on it!"

I surprise hug him. "Thank you."

He squeezes me before extracting himself from my arms. "Okay, okay. Don't get all mushy on me. You know I'm always here for you."

I hurry out to my car, rummaging around in my trunk until I find the box with the spray.

Danny reads the description and chuckles. "Take me to the twerp's smell-good stuff!"

We rush into the bathroom and Danny grabs his cologne while I read the instructions out loud.

"Okay, leave about 1/4 of the cologne in the bottle. Then fill the rest with the Sneaky-Stinky stuff. Apparently, it will smell like the cologne until it doesn't."

Danny is laughing so hard that he can barely pour without making a mess. Then he grabs Trevor's body wash and dumps the rest in.

I hustle to the hall closet to grab my toolbox and start taking down the curtains. I shove a handful of shrimp into each rod and reattach them to the windows. Danny strolls in, grinning, holding what looks like every battery in the house in a plastic container.

"What's next, boss lady?"

"We're going to open up the vents and put the salmon in there. There's a step stool in the kitchen, then I'm really not sure what else to do," I reply.

"Reset the router password so he has to call customer service to get the internet working again," Danny gleefully orders me.

"I don't know how to do that. I'll hide his gaming controllers, you reset the password."

"No! Don't hide his controllers yet. Can I screw with them?" he asks with puppy dog eyes.

"Yes. Please. What are you thinking?"

"Well, I could re-map all of them and then we hide them. Really fuck with him."

"What's re-mapping?" I ask.

"Basically it's going into the console settings and making the buttons on his controller do something different than they're supposed to. It's super easy to do but hard to undo if you don't know what buttons are what. Either that or he would have to go buy a new controller. Either way, sucks for him."

"Oh, he would hate that so much!" I cheer.

"And while you were busy, I poured bleach into his laundry detergent."

"You're my favorite brother!" I say, hugging him again.

***

"We should go back and take the furniture, too," Danny says, setting the last boxes down in my new loft apartment.

"I don't want a single piece of furniture in that house. I don't want anything that he bought or might have fucked a girl on."

Danny scrunches his face in disgust. "I didn't think about that."

"That's why I'm the brains of this operation."

"The stupid brains," he snarks, sticking his tongue out.

"No, you are!"

"Children!" Mom says, glaring at us like we're five again.

My dad rubs her shoulder. "Oh, let the kids play, Mama."

"Five more minutes then we need to calm down. It's almost dinner time," Mom says, making us all laugh.

"Speaking of." Dad claps his hands. "What kind of grub are we thinking for tonight? Probably a sit-down kind of place since our girl doesn't have a stick of furniture. Then we gotta run by the storage place and pick up your bed and those new sheets and shit."

"You don't have to do that, I can get the bed and stuff when you all leave."

"Nonsense, I'm making sure my baby girl is alright before I go home."

"Thanks, Papa Bear." I giggle, throwing my arms around him.

***

I'm finally completely alone in my new house. It's a free-standing loft apartment. One big rectangle of a room with the kitchen, dining area, and living room with a full bath under the loft. The bedroom is visible at the top of the stairs.

I love being able to see the rest of the house from my bed—that'll make me feel more secure staying here alone. I've never lived alone before. I went straight from my parent's home to college dorms and then to living with Trevor. I'm nervous but so excited for this new chapter in my life. I can't wait to start hitting the thrift stores. Decorating this place is going to be a blast!

The neighborhood is super cute, too. Outside the center of town, a few minutes from the hotel and beach, sits a precious little neighborhood consisting of tiny cottages called Dandelion Haven. The cottage I rent is baby blue with light yellow shutters and trim. I'm in love with this area and so excited to be living in Verbania, my safe place during this whole ordeal.

After Bennett and I checked out all of the open rentals in town I couldn't figure out what to do. Live in a house I don't love in a town that I do love? Find a place that I love in a town that I don't love? Both felt like settling and I'm done with that nonsense. Luckily, a few days after the rental tour the nice realtor lady called and informed me of a new spot. This one. And it's perfect. I can't wait to show Bennett, since he is the whole reason I'm here. If he hadn't been with me, I would definitely be moving into a baby poop colored house.

I can't help but smile as I look around my loft. White walls and hardwood floors, I have a few boxes of my tchotchkes, books, and clothes in the corner of the otherwise empty living space. The only pieces of furniture are the thrift store bed and a new mattress upstairs. I dig through a couple of boxes until I find my old laptop and stash of DVDs. Gathering my takeout cheesecake, I haul the whole thing up to my sleeping space. I set up the laptop on my bed and pop in one of my favorite movies. Making myself cozy in my new bedding and pushing play, I take a bite of cheesecake and shoot a text over to Bennett, including a photo of my empty house.

> **Betty: Finally moved in with my 6 boxes of knick-knacks and new bed.**

> **Bennett: Looks great! Do you need me to bring you some furniture?**

> **Betty: LOL You're sweet. But I'm excited to shop and fill it with exactly what I want.**

> **Bennett: It will be lovely when you finish. I'm pretty busy for the rest of the week but would love to see you. Would you like to eat take-out in my office with me at noon tomorrow?**

Betty: YES! I'll pick us up some burgers and meet you there!

Bennett: You don't have to. I can have something delivered.

Betty: Nonsense. I'll already be out and about, I can grab something.

Bennett: If you insist.

Betty: I do.

Bennett: I will see you tomorrow. Congratulations on the new place.

Betty: Thank you! See you tomorrow!

Thirteen

Betty

I ADJUST MY BLACK cigarette pants and make sure my blouse is lying correctly before grabbing the takeout from my car. I hope I don't run into Trevor—not that he would cause a scene, but it would be unbearably awkward. The front receptionist checks the visitor list and upon finding my name, sends me up to the top floor. Once the elevator passes the third floor, where Trevor's office is, I breathe a sigh of relief.

That relief deflates when I realize that Paige—the Paige my ex-husband has been screwing—is Bennett's receptionist. She looks surprised to see me and cuts her eyes over to the restroom before asking, "How can I help you?"

Before I can open my mouth to answer, Trevor meanders out of the restroom adjusting his tie and stops abruptly when he notices me. I set the greasy bag of burgers on Paige's desk, needing my hands free for this conversation. He looks around to verify no one else is within earshot before saying, "What the fuck are you doing here? I told you to leave me alone. We aren't getting back together."

I'm taken aback, and Paige gives me a superior look, as if she won a prize.

I force myself to laugh. "What are you talking about? I left *you*."

"You said that *you* left *her!*" Paige exclaims, trying to grab Trevor's hand.

Trevor ignores her and grabs my arm. "What are you doing here?"

"Let go of me." I yank my arm, stumbling back into a solid wall of muscle. Trevor's face pales as strong arms reach around me and a kiss lands on my head.

"Is there a problem?" Bennett asks, letting me go to step in front.

I can't help but giggle as I slide my arm into his. Trevor's eyes immediately snap to where I am touching Bennett, his face turning an alarming shade of red.

"Why are you fucking touching my wife?" he shouts at Bennett.

Paige's face blanches—she obviously had no idea Trevor didn't want to let me go. Of course, he would lie to her. A worm of sympathy wiggles in but I squash it quickly, she knew he was married.

"I'm not touching your wife. I'm touching *my girlfriend.* You are nothing to her," Bennett growls.

That is when Trevor loses his shit.

He rushes up and yanks me away with his left hand and throws a punch at Bennett's jaw with his right. Paige is screaming, executives are coming out of their offices, and the area devolves into chaos.

Bennett picks me up and moves me away from Trevor before snatching him up by the collar and walking him backward into the wall.

"You will never lay a finger on her again," he snarls, inches from the twerp's face.

"Ye-yes, s-s-sir," Trevor stutters, face pale at the fury on Bennett's face.

"Good. You're fired." Bennett gives him one last shake and turns immediately to me.

I find myself starstruck. Bennett, my friend Bennett, is really hot with protective rage in his eyes. I need to shake that shit off.

Just friends.

Just friends.

He rushes up to me, pulling me into his arms, and I meet him halfway, our lips crashing together.

Oh.

Oh my god.

Why haven't we been doing this the whole time?

All too soon he pulls back, his eyes nervously searching mine, and I grin at him. He smiles a rare smile back at me and my heart skips a beat.

Then the chaos seeps back into our consciousness and we pull apart, eyes still locked.

"You said *you* didn't want *her*!" Paige yells in Trevor's face as he sputters out apologies.

"Lukas, call security. Have them escort Trevor out," Bennett says.

Lukas nods and rushes away. Trevor can't take his eyes off of me, Paige is still yelling in his face, and Bennett takes my hand and leads me into his office.

"I'm sorry for kissing you out there."

My stomach lurches. Of course. That kiss was a mistake. My heart drops into my shoes, and tears prick my eyes. This is fine. Of course he didn't mean to kiss me like that. We are just friends and...

"I should have waited until now," he finishes, caging me against the door.

His lips catch mine, and I see fireworks. It's lips and teeth, fire and passion. He kisses me like I am the air he needs to breathe.

He pulls back, breathing hard. "Is this okay? Can I touch you?"

He can do whatever he wants to me. "Yes, please."

He brings his lips to mine, slowly, so softly. As if he is savoring me. His hands lightly brush down my sides to grip my hips as his mouth moves against mine.

We jump apart when Paige knocks on his door. "Sir? Your lunch is still sitting out here."

Bennett gently moves me as I watch his face change from dreamy to stern and he opens the door. Paige stands on the other side, her eyes puffy, holding our bag of burgers. Bennett looks at me and says, "Betty, would you please step out for a second? I need to speak with Ms. Barker."

Paige looks nervous as I slip by her and out the door. My insecurities rise to the surface, after all this is the woman that my husband would rather be with. *Ex-husband.* What if Bennett wants her, too? No, don't be ridiculous. Trevor is such a twerp, Bennett is nothing like him.

Even so, nausea hits me. How long should this take? Is she seducing him? No. Bennett would not do that, even if we stay just friends.

I breathe in and out, slowly, until the nausea subsides. *I'm okay.*

Bennett's door flings open, startling me. Paige rushes out of the room, tears streaming down her face, and angrily starts stuffing her bag with items from her desk. She glares at me as if any of this is my fault. I walk back into Bennett's office.

"Well, that was unexpected." I laugh, slumping into one of the chairs by the window.

His eyes snap over to meet mine, a smirk on his face. "Very unexpected."

Heat pools in my stomach. Is Bennett sexy? He's always been handsome but seeing him put Trevor in his place was pretty damn sexy. And here, with a smirk and fire in his eyes? Bennett Sterling is *hot.*

"So..." I say, accepting the burger that Bennett hands me.

He looks at me, looks away, looks at me, and opens his mouth—

Ding

Bennett glances at his phone and then looks at me, torn.

"It's okay. I knew you were busy today. I'll go ahead and leave so you can get back to work."

He smiles at me, obviously relieved, and says, "I am so sorry that our time together was ruined but thank you for being understanding. I have a meeting to get to or I would at least walk you out."

"No worries, babycakes, make yo money, but you need to make sure you eat." I gesture to our now cold burgers and fries.

"I will," he says.

I tiptoe up, kiss his cheek, and hustle out of his office—fully aware that every eye is on me. I hope they don't gossip too much. But I do add an extra sway to my step so when they gossip they have something good to say. In the elevator, I press the parking level button and try to ignore the sinking feeling in my stomach. Trevor. What the hell is wrong with him? He has a whole girlfriend why is he worried about me?

I have to be grateful that he will be out of my life very soon.

But Bennett, oh holy cow. What am I going to do about him? What do I want to do about him? Maybe even more importantly, what does he want to do with me?

***

Bennett

My hands shake as I watch Betty saunter out of my office.

I collapse down into my chair. Adrenaline rushes from my body as the last hour catches up to me. The eager anticipation I felt knowing that Betty was going to stop by turned into rage as I watched her husband lay his hands on her. Then the need to touch Betty, kiss Betty. I've never felt so many emotions at once. It was terrifying and exhilarating.

I have an erection—which isn't newsworthy but I've never gotten one in response to another person. Betty. Her lush lips on mine, my hands on her hips. How do I go about my day knowing how she feels against me?

My heart is pounding, my penis is hard, and I can't stop thinking about Betty.

I need to compartmentalize. And quickly, my meeting starts in less than ten minutes.

Pulling out my pocket notebook, I write out all of these feelings and ideas so I can think about them later.

I kissed Betty.

Betty kissed me back and smiled at me. And kissed my cheek.

Betty let me touch her body.

I might be in love with her.

I desire Betty.

I shoved an employee against the wall. I think I liked it.

Feeling better—but not normal—I shakily gather my files. I should cancel this meeting but Sterlings don't let our personal lives interfere with business. I read over my notes, willing my penis to behave like a gentleman, and control my breathing.

I'm startled out of my notes when Lukas says, "Mr. Sterling?" after knocking on the door.

"Come in."

"Sir, your appointment is here. I put them in the conference room, I hope that's okay? There was no one out here to greet them."

I cannot believe I so quickly forgot about firing my receptionist.

"That is perfect. Thank you."

He flushes before saying, "You're welcome. Is there anything else I can do for you?"

"Would you mind standing in for my receptionist for the rest of the day? If your own tasks won't fall behind, of course."

"I don't mind at all. I can fill in for Paige for as long as you need me to," he replies, smiling.

"Thank you."

Taking a deep breath, I shift into business mode.

***

Betty

Hands shaking, I sit in my car, thinking about Bennett. Sweet, honest, and totally hot Bennett.

I need to talk about this.

I put my phone on speaker, calling Lilith, before getting on the road to Verbania.

"Betty! What's up?"

"So much! Trevor and Bennett got into a fight and I kissed Bennett! Help!"

"Holy cow. Um, was it good? Shit. Where are you? Can you come over?"

"Yes! Please! I'm coming back from Coslada, so maybe an hour? Want to see my new loft?"

"Yes! Text me when you get home and I'll come running!"

The drive home speeds by in a blur. I keep replaying the events of today, over and over. I'm confused, a little aroused, and very relieved.

I slow the car once I reach my new neighborhood. Carefully checking the house numbers—I would hate to walk into the wrong loft—I pull into my lucky number thirteen.

I text Lilith and sit on my front porch step, mind reeling.

Within moments I hear Lilith squeal. "Betty! Tell me everything!"

She jogs up my stairs, her purple denim overalls rasping softly as she sits next to me. I lean over and lay my head on her shoulder, covered by a soft fuzzy sweater.

Sighing, I sit up and say, "I don't even know where to begin. Everything happened so fast, it's all a blur."

She nudges me with her knee and wiggles her eyebrows. "Well, start with the best part. Is Bennett a tiger under all his suits and encyclopedias?"

Laughing, I nod and fan myself. "Oh, that he is."

Lilith claps, then throws her arms around me, squeezing me tight. "I just knew he would be! I have been waiting on this for ages! You guys took forever!"

"Forever? I don't even know what this is! We just kissed. Probably got caught up in the moment, you know?"

"You are so silly. Of course, you kissing Bennett is more than getting caught up. I bet that was your last first kiss, better do like Benny and write this shit down!"

Giggling, I cover my face with my hands. "You really think so?"

"Duh. Now tell me about this fight. Sounds hot."

"It was so not hot! Okay, well, Bennett was totally hot. But everything else was weird and scary. Like, what the fuck was Trevor even thinking?"

Lilith shrugs one pink, fuzzy-sweater clad shoulder. "I dunno. You haven't even told me what happened."

"Right, right." I huff in disbelief. "Okay. So, I'm going to eat with Bennett, right? In his office. I figure I can just slide by Trevor's floor and not see him, but Paige is Bennett's assistant!"

"*The* Paige? The dirty, rotten husband-fucker? And she called douchebag up?"

"Yes! I mean—no—she didn't call him up there. He was already up there!"

Lilith scrunches her nose. "Ew."

"Right? And after all of his crying the other night, he looks me straight in the face and tells me I need to leave *him* alone! That he doesn't want *me* anymore! I was freaking flabbergasted!"

"The balls on that bastard!"

"I know, right? So, I'm all like, I left *you*, motherfucker—but I don't say motherfucker, of course. Then Trevor grabs my arm and Bennett is there, and Trevor tries to punch him! To punch Bennett!"

"Just out of nowhere?" Lilith gasps, shaking her hands.

"Oh! No! Bennett told him to get his hands off *his* girlfriend! Called me his girlfriend to my stupid husband's face!"

"Holy shit."

"I know!"

"Well?" Lilith asks, eyes wide. "He tries to punch Bennett, and what? Bennett punches him back?"

"No, that's what was so hot. Bennett just grabs his shirt and pushes him against the wall. Just controlled the situation—all powerful and shit."

"Wow," she breathes out.

"I know!" I giggle, then the weight of the day crashes into me. "But why would Trevor—why would he do that? He was up there talking to Paige, obviously. Why won't he just leave me alone?"

"Because he's greedy."

Nothing left to say, we sit with the salty breeze whipping our hair around.

Fourteen

Betty

BENNETT AND I ARE sitting on the floor with our backs against the wall. "Want to come with me to the thrift store in a little bit?"

"I would love to. Are we furnishing your new home?"

"Yep!" I chirp, getting excited to finally visit *Seaside Treasures*. I've glanced in the windows numerous times but haven't had the chance to actually go poke around.

Banging on my front door makes both of us jump. "Betty! I need to talk to you! I know you're here, I see your car!"

Trevor.

"How did he know where I live?" I whisper to Bennett, who is looking furious.

"I don't know but I'm going to find out," Bennett snarls, pushing up to his feet.

"Wait, let me see what he wants before you go all alpha on me. Will you sit tight and let me handle it?"

Bang. Bang. Bang.

"Bethany!" Trevor yells again.

"I will. But if he insults or threatens you, I will not allow it," Bennett says, standing up and leaning against the wall where he won't be seen from the front door.

I sigh, open my front door, and quickly step outside on the porch. I don't want Trevor in my new home.

"What the fuck, Bethany?" Trevor glares as I stand there with my arms crossed.

"What the fuck what, Trevor?" I ask, exasperated.

"You move out, have me served with divorce papers, and then show up to fuck my boss and get me and my girlfriend fired!"

"Yes, yes, of course I did. I did all of that just to fuck with you. But how did you know where I live?" I reply.

"You are my wife!" He yells.

"Only until the divorce is finalized. How did you know where I live?"

"I know you've been fucking him! Fucking Bennett Sterling!"

"That's none of your business. How did you know where I moved to?" I yell the last part, done with his bullshit.

"I had to hire a fucking investigator. To find my fucking whore of a wife," he sneers.

My front door slams open, Bennett looking furious in my doorway.

"Go inside, please, Betty."

A shiver runs down my spine—an angry Bennett is a very sexy Bennett.

"I'm okay," I tell him, putting a hand on his chest.

He covers it with his hand and looks down at me. "Please go inside. I will handle things with Mr. Smith."

I shrug, not like I *wanted* to deal with Trevor anyway, and strut back into my house. I'm not sure what Bennett and I are doing with each other but whatever it is, I like it.

***

Bennett

I stand there, glaring at the bastard and making him nervous, until Betty is inside and the door shut. She doesn't need to see this.

Before a word can fly out of his slimy mouth, my fist connects to his jaw with a crunch. He starts falling backward, but I grab his shirt and sling him into the closed front door. Holding him with a hand on his throat, I look into his sniveling face and say, "Stay away from Betty. Sign the divorce papers, and forget her address. You betrayed that woman and now she's mine. And you better believe that I won't fuck up."

I shake him, his head banging against the door before shoving him away from the cottage. I cross my arms and watch as he limps to his sports car, jumps inside, and screeches out of the driveway—his tires slipping on the gravel.

The adrenaline is rushing through my veins and I want to run or go to the gym, something active. But then Betty is there, jumping into my arms, her legs around my waist and her mouth on mine. My hands are on her bottom. This is amazing.

This is so much better than going to the gym.

I carry her inside, and she slides down my front until her ruffled sock-clad feet hit the floor. My mouth is still on hers, she tastes like happiness. I break our kiss, both of us breathing heavily, to sit down and pull her into my lap.

Then I kiss her again.

***

Betty

Bennett feels so good against me, I wish I had worn a dress today. I wiggle in his lap and he smiles against my lips as he ends the kiss. A couple more pecks on the lips and he pulls back, his hands still on my ass.

He clears his throat. "I need to sort you out some security for this place."

That is not quite what I had expected him to say after that kiss.

"Oh, um. Don't, don't worry about it. I'll handle it, do you have a company that you recommend?"

"Please allow me to set it up."

I tilt my shoulders. "Okay."

He laughs, pulls out his phone, and says, "I've got a security guy. Let me call him."

I try to climb off Bennett's lap so he can make his call, but he grips my ass tighter and mouths, *stay*.

"Robin, this is Bennett Sterling. I have an urgent need for home security. Please call me back at your earliest convenience. Thank you."

He hangs up the phone and pats my ass. "I think we should always sit like this."

I giggle and lay my head on his shoulder.

"I agree," I murmur into his neck.

He rubs his hands up and down my back. "Would you like to discuss our current relationship now or after we go thrifting? I do feel that we should discuss it today."

I smile against his neck and say, "You told Trevor that I was yours. Seems like we skipped the discussion."

I lean back so I can see his face as he smiles and replies, "Yes, I did say that. However, the choice is entirely yours. I would like to enter a relationship with you. I find myself quite attracted to and possessive of you. You already know that I greatly enjoy your company."

I shimmy my shoulders, "You just want to kiss me and grope my booty more."

"Yes, I very much would like to do that more. But I also want to take you on dates, to charity galas, and wherever you want to go. I would like to do many things while holding your hand."

My heart races as his words find their way into my heart and I place my hands on his reddened cheeks saying, "I would like to do all of that with you, too."

His smile is blinding before he claims my lips again.

***

Hand in hand we walk to *Seaside Treasures*, sun on our faces and salt in the air. Today was so dramatic, I'm glad Bennett was with me when Trevor showed up. Trevor might have been an asshole while we were married but he was never aggressive until recently.

He's pulling the shop's door open when his phone rings. Raising my hand to his lips, he presses a kiss and says, "It's my security guy. I need to take this. Do you mind?"

"Not a bit, I'll meet you inside," I reply, my hand all tingly and my heart giggly.

"Robin, how are you? Good, listen..." Bennett says into the phone before the shop door closes.

Warmth spreads through my chest, I'm going to fall hard for this man.

I cannot believe that Trevor hired someone to find me. Why does he even care so much? Never in all of the years that I've known him would I believe he would unravel this way. Away from Bennett, breathing in the comforting scent of stale books, the past few days catch up with me.

What the actual hell? Trevor threw a punch at his boss, his boss whom he thought I was dating. Paige was Bennett's assistant and he fired her. Trevor showed up at my house to what? Get me back? Call me names? What would he have done if Bennett hadn't been there?

What would he have done if Bennett hadn't been there?

I stare at the knick-knack in front of me, trying to focus on anything other than my racing heart. I'm so overwhelmed, I need to get out of here. I can't breathe.

The world starts to narrow, and darkness seeps in but before it pulls me under Bennett is there, pulling me out.

"Breathe. In and out." He exaggerates his breathing.

"Can we," I start, trying to gather myself. "Can we just go home?"

"Of course, mine or yours? I would rather take you to mine since you have no furniture."

"Yours, please."

***

Bennett

Betty slept the entire ride to Coslada. I should look into getting a home in Verbania to be closer to her. I rush up to unlock my front door before gently pulling Betty into my arms—careful not to wake her.

That bastard should thank his lucky stars that he didn't lay a finger on her. I felt enough fury to put him in the hospital—which would very negatively affect my life.

I lay her on my sofa and Stella covers her with a throw blanket. Thank goodness for Stella—I didn't even know that I had throw blankets. We walk into the kitchen and Stella silently starts a pot of coffee. I sit at the table and put my head in my hands.

"What happened to chicky?" Stella asks, setting a mug of coffee in front of me.

"Her almost-ex-husband showed up at her new house and caused a scene."

"Bennett, baby, just this once could you tell me the whole story without me having to pull it from you?"

"Yes. I think I can do that," I say. Then I tell Stella the situation, starting three days ago at my office and ending with Betty on my sofa. Excluding the kissing, of course.

"Well, shit. That fucker. I can make some calls, really scare the little shithead." Stella offers.

"While tempting, perhaps we should let Betty make that decision."

"You're probably right about that." She stands up. "I'm going to cook dinner and then you can wake her up and feed her. I'm guessing you have a plan for an alarm or something at her house?"

"Yes, I spoke with Robin and he has someone coming out tomorrow afternoon."

"Good, good. That's all that can be done right now. Alright, then."

Stella turns and opens the fridge, muttering to herself about comfort food and pulling ingredients. That means it is time for me to leave the kitchen, she always complains if she can see me while cooking. Apparently, I get 'under her feet.'

Unsure of what to do, I walk back into the living room to check on Betty. She is so beautiful—her face relaxed, her make-up smudged. Yogurt has curled up in her arms. I don't know what I am going to do with this vibrant woman. How can I keep her happy? I've never had a relationship. I've never even dated.

But the mere idea of letting another man touch her sends jealousy radiating down my skin. It makes me want to grab her and demand that she never look at anyone but me.

I don't do that.

Because I'm a gentleman.

But I do open my Sterling Shop app and look up her pen name, Tilda Vaughn, and purchase every single book she has ever written. In e-book and paperback. I can study how she wants to be loved through the books she has written on love.

I can also make a spreadsheet of the sex moves in her books and find out exactly what she wants in bed. Yes. That is what I will do.

I settle in the armchair next to the sofa, where I can watch over Betty as she rests. I pull up the Sterling Shop reading app and download her very first book, *His Good Girl.* Not my usual read—I'm more of a nonfiction man, but for her, anything.

I get three chapters in when the first sex scene occurs, I open my notebook and start taking notes. Sweating, I open my collar. I've never felt sexual attraction like this before. As I read I keep picturing Betty and I in the positions she wrote. Is that one even possible? Can women fold like that? I don't know, but I want to try it.

My hands shake, making my writing unsteady, but there is no calming my racing heart. I put a throw pillow on my lap to cover my pulsing erection. I'm uncomfortable and hot, but never want to stop. I see why books like this sell so well—Betty really is talented.

"Bennett, you okay? You're really red," Betty murmurs, her voice thick with sleep.

"Oh, um, yes. Quite alright," I say, adjusting the pillow I'm now very glad that I placed in my lap.

"Are you sure?"

"Of course, but how are you?"

She looks at me, head tilted, and replies, "I feel way better. Sorry for freaking out on you."

I close my reading app and place the notebook on the end table before sitting beside Betty on the couch, moving her feet onto my lap pillow. Hopefully, taking care of Betty will help me survive this predicament without embarrassing myself. I don't even know if she wants to have sex with me, but now is definitely not the time to broach the subject. That thought does a lot to help my erection go down.

"Never apologize to me for having a panic attack. You couldn't help it, and even if you could—if you need to panic then panic."

"Thank you," she says, chewing on her bottom lip. She's not quite making eye contact with me, which feels decidedly not like Betty.

I lean toward her, trying to decipher her body language and failing.

"What is the matter? Do you need something?"

She covers her face with her hands and mumbles, "I'm so embarrassed."

Surprised, I ask, "What about?"

"I just, like, collapsed like a stupid damsel in distress. And you had to take care of me. I ruined the whole day with my bullshit—first Trevor, and then freaking out." She groans from behind her hands.

I reach out and tug at her until she ends up in my lap, laughing.

"I don't have any experience in relationships, but isn't that what a couple is supposed to do? Take care of each other? I like being the one who gets to take care of you."

She lays her head on my shoulder before saying, "Yes, but we just became a thing. Like, we became girlfriend and boyfriend, and then I immediately panic and pass out. That is so not a great start."

"I agree that you panicking isn't great—simply because you were distressed and I never want you to be unhappy. But this isn't our start. We began when you saved me from that woman at the bar. Our relationship started then, to me."

She leans back, patting my chest. "Yes! To me, too! Okay. You aren't upset with me? You can tell me if you are."

"I will never be upset with you because of a panic attack—or any emotions you might experience. I want to be the person you turn to when you are feeling out of control or sad. I want to take on your burdens."

"Stop, or I'll cry," she says, smiling at me, eyes shining. "Oh my god! I must look terrifying!" Betty jumps up and rushes down the hall to the bathroom.

Stella pops out from around the corner. "She doing better?"

"Yes, I believe so. Is dinner ready?"

"It is. I'm fixing to head out. Now then, I got a bone to pick with you. I told you to tell me everything, and you didn't say a damn thing about you two becoming an item. Lap sitting and everything."

"Well, I, uh, it didn't seem appropriate to bring it up at that time."

"Maybe not. Either way, good for you. I was hoping this would happen. Couple sweet baby angels doing sweet baby angel things."

"Oh. Yes, thank you." I stammer, unsure of the correct reply to end this conversation before Betty returns.

Stella laughs. "Tell chicky that I'll see her later. I better scram and let y'all be alone."

"Thank you for dinner. It smells delicious."

"Anytime, baby angel."

The front door clicks shut as Betty emerges from the bathroom, her face bare of makeup and her eyes a little puffy. *Simply stunning.*

"Stella cooked comfort food for you. Shall we eat?"

"Yes, please. I'm starving! Is Stella still here?" Betty says, walking toward the kitchen.

"No, she left while you were in the bathroom. She wanted me to tell you that she'll see you later but she thought that we would want to be alone."

"Did you tell her about us?" She asks, a hint of unease in her voice.

"I did. Should I not have?" I reply.

Have I done something wrong?

"Oh no! I'm glad you did! I just wasn't sure if you wanted people to know we are together yet."

Shock ripples down my spine. "I would like everyone to know that we are together as soon as possible. Why wouldn't I want people to know we are dating?"

Her eyes fill with tears as she shrugs and says, "I'm sorry. I shouldn't compare you to Trevor, and I don't mean to. I just, he didn't want to tell people that we were together at first. And I got worried that maybe you didn't. I'm sorry, you're nothing like Trevor and I know that."

I pull her to me and silence her ramblings with a kiss. A kiss that I meant to be simple and sweet but it turns passionate quickly, leaving us both breathless when I pull away.

"Never apologize for feeling what you feel. I want to know every feeling you've ever had—bad or good. We are partners now. Let me be here for you. And compare me to Trevor all you want, it's not me that you will find lacking."

She laughs, as I hoped she would, and lets me lead her into the dining room.

***

Betty

Meatloaf. Stella made meatloaf.

Why does meatloaf always show up when everything is falling apart?

"Would you like me to plate your food?" Bennett asks.

What do I do? Eat the fucking meatloaf?

Stella went through so much trouble to make a nice dinner.

My eyes prick with tears. *Oh no.* I can't cry over a gross meal. A gross meal that someone cooked for me.

How ungrateful can you be?

I take a deep breath, willing my eyes to chill out.

"Betty?" Bennett says my name with such concern that I can't stop the tears from falling.

"I'm sorry." I wail.

"What's wrong? What can I do?" He asks, a hint of panic in his voice. He picks me up and sits me on the counter, his hazel eyes searching my face for any sign of why I'm crying.

"I'm sorry."

Say something else, you dumb broad.

"No more apologies, please. I can not bear it. Cry all you want, all you need. I'm here. Can you tell me what's wrong?"

Sniffling, I say, "I hate meatloaf—the food. I love Meat Loaf the singer."

Thank you for clarifying.

"I'm the one who is sorry, I should have checked with you before Stella started cooking."

"No, no. This is such a nice thing and once again, I ruined it," I sob.

"Betty. Listen to me. Your feelings will never ruin anything. I might not understand why meatloaf-the-food brings you to tears but I will endeavor to never let meatloaf in the same room as you again."

That startles a watery chuckle out of me. I take a deep breath, dreading mentioning my ex-husband again, but wanting Bennett to understand that I'm not crying over a dinner.

"So, on that night. Our fifth anniversary... mine and Trevor's, when he asked for the open marriage. He wanted meatloaf, it's his favorite but I've never particularly cared for it. So my husband told me that he didn't find me attractive anymore over meatloaf."

"I would like to punch him again." Bennett growls, gathering me in his arms and kissing the top of my head. I wrap my legs around his waist, needing to be closer to him. *I wish we were naked.*

"Thank you."

He doesn't say anything, just squeezes me tighter as if he is holding all of my pieces together. And maybe he is.

My tears cease and I give Bennett one last squeeze before leaning away acutely aware of how I must look to him. He's so handsome and put together and I—well, I probably look like a red pufferfish at this point.

He tucks a loose strand of hair behind my ear.

"You are so pretty," he says so reverently that I almost believe him.

Fifteen

Betty

BENNETT IS TAKING ME on a surprise date! I can't stop dancing around my apartment, trying on everything I own. I settle on a leopard print pencil skirt with a black off-shoulder top and a wide red belt. Matching wedges, lots of curls, and red lipstick complete the outfit.

Is it too much? Should I switch to a black skirt?

I don't know. Maybe I should cancel the date. Go shopping.

Breathe in.

Breathe out.

Alright, I strike a pose and snap a picture, sending it to my brother.

> If a chick showed up for a first date dressed like this, would you ghost her?

He replies immediately.

> Probably. But that's because she looks just like my sister. If a guy is taking you out and you show up like that he better be fucking thrilled.

I laugh at his reply. Of course he'd say that. But it *does* make me feel better. Bennett knows what he's getting into. Why try to cover who I am?

But to be safe, I also send the picture to Lilith.

> First real date with Bennett. Too much?

I turn the music up and take myself on a waltz until I hear that familiar chime.

> NOT AT ALL!!!!!!!HOT!!!!!!!

I throw myself onto the bed, giggling. I want to roll around and kick my feet but can't risk wrinkling my outfit.

***

Bennett

My palms are sweating and my heart is hammering against my ribs as I pull into Betty's driveway. I've never been on a romantic date before—this is going to be a disaster.

A train ride and a picnic? I should have made reservations at the best restaurant in Coslada. That is what she deserves, the very best. Not some train ride and eating on the ground. I glance at the brand-new picnic basket that Stella assured me would please Betty.

Despite my doubts, it is too late to change anything. I'm sure Betty heard me pull up, and she would be quite upset with me if I canceled now.

I never want to cause her displeasure.

***

Betty

I barely hear Bennett's soft knock over Britney Spears blaring from my Bluetooth speaker. I squeak softly as I shimmy to turn off the music and bounce down the loft stairs to the front door.

I fling open the door and my jaw hits the floor. Bennett looks ridiculously gorgeous in his perfectly tailored dark gray slacks and a deep green button-down shirt, with the sleeves rolled up to expose his sexy forearms.

"You are stunning," Bennett says, looking as awestruck as I feel.

"No, you are!" I say, giggling.

Bennett gives me a sexy little smile that makes my heart flutter. I grab my shiny red pleather bag and leap into his arms, kissing him on the cheek. My red lipstick smudges on his face, and I panic a little. "Oh no! I'm sorry, I got lipstick all over you!"

He smiles brightly. "Shall I leave it there so everyone knows you kissed me?"

I could cry—he's so wonderful.

"No, no, let me wipe it off," I say, hustling to my bathroom for a makeup wipe.

His eyes are kind as he patiently waits for me to clean his face. My pulse pounds—I'm falling hard for this man.

After I finish my task and dispose of the wipe, Bennett offers me his arm and leads me to the car. He opens the door and helps me in before rushing around to sit next to me.

"I didn't take you for a guy who has a driver," I whisper, giggling.

There is that little grin again. "I don't usually, but we won't need the car long. I wanted to be able to focus completely on you today."

My heart squeezes almost painfully.

We talk nonsense the whole drive. Well, I talk nonsense and Bennett listens. Really listens.

I hate that I keep comparing Bennett to Trevor, but damn. I was married to a man for five years who never listened to me with the intensity that Bennett does. Bennett listens like he needs my words to survive—even when I am rambling on about finding a bag to match a particular pair of hot pink shoes.

"Could you send me a photo of the shoes? And photos of the styles of bags you enjoy. Perhaps I can help."

"Oh, no, I'll eventually find one. It's not a big deal or anything," I reply, thrilled that he wants to help.

"I enjoy tracking down hard-to-find items. Probably why I enjoy collecting encyclopedias so much."

"Well, if you insist," I say, pulling my phone out to send him the pictures.

He pulls out his pocket notebook and jots something down as his phone chimes out this fun, sparkly sound.

"That's a new notification noise!"

"I like knowing that it's you texting me. It took me an hour to find a tone that sounded like you," he replies, bashfully.

***

We stop at this gorgeous train station called Darlington Railway. It's all 1950s retro, and I am in love. I cannot believe that this has been in San Remo this whole time and I've never visited!

I'm vibrating with excitement as Bennett gets a picnic basket out of the trunk and takes my hand. This is marvelous!

"Is there a spot to picnic here?" I ask, looking around. It's a bit early for lunch, but I always love a little snack.

He grins and replies, "I don't think so. We are taking a train ride and then will have a picnic along the way, if that is acceptable to you?"

"Seriously?" I ask. "This is the best date ever!"

He lets out a puff of air, looking relieved, and says, "I am glad that you approve."

"Oh, I do! I do!" I say, dragging him into the building.

It's a gift shop! I love gift shops—cheap souvenirs thrill me. I squeeze Bennett's hand a couple of times and then let go so I can look at the trinkets. Train snow globes, t-shirts, and tiny spoons—oh my.

"Oh, I have to get a snow globe, but I can't decide. Which one do you like better?" I turn to Bennett, holding out two nearly identical snow globes. But one has a green base and the other has a red base.

He carefully inspects each one before replying, "I think the green one, the train is more prominent. However, would you like to wait until after our train ride? We are due to board in ten minutes."

"Oh! Yes! And we won't have to lug my goodies around all day!"

"I am more than willing to carry your items," he says, taking my hand and leading me to board the train.

The train car is magnificent—burgundy with deep green and royal blue velvet accents, lush and luxurious. I want to lay on everything and roll around but that wouldn't be first-date appropriate. Maybe for our third date.

"Bennett! This is just fantastic!"

"It really is, isn't it?" he replies, looking around.

"Which seat is ours?"

"I rented this whole car, so whichever seat you want is yours," he says, looking nervous.

"Seriously? That is awesome! This is so much fun—have I told you that this is the best date ever? Because it is. Best. Date. Ever!"

He gives me that little smile that makes my knees go weak and says, "I'm glad that you approve. I worried that you would not enjoy this outing and would rather have a restaurant dinner. In fact, I almost canceled this to take you to Rosette. Stella talked me out of it and I am very pleased that she did."

I laugh. "I don't know anything about Rosette except it's super fancy, but please thank Stella for me. She was so right to talk you out of it. I've never even been to a real fancy restaurant."

"I will relay the message," Bennett says, as the car attendant tells us to have a seat—we should be moving momentarily.

***

Bennett, our picnic basket on one arm and my hand in his, leads me to a lovely open field with a perfect view of this fairy wonderland that we've found ourselves in. The train station almost melts into the scenery, as if it belongs. There is a stream that ends at a small lake and brilliantly colored flowers everywhere. I know that if we are still enough, we will be covered in butterflies and watching deer frolic or whatever deer do.

I tug him closer to the lake and find the perfect spot to have lunch. Like the other passengers, we spread out our blanket and settle the basket and ourselves.

"Benny! This place is like a dream! I don't think I'll ever want to leave!"

He smiles brightly and says, "I can arrange for you to stay here as long as you want."

Giggling, I pat his hand and reply, "You can't just snap your fingers and give me anything I want."

He raises a sexy eyebrow. "Actually, I can. And I intend to. You deserve to have everything you want."

"Dating a gazillionaire is so bizarre. You can, can't you? Just do whatever you want, really?"

"Within reason, but yes. I never do—but for you? Nothing is beyond your reach. I would love to spoil you," he says, a small smile on his red face.

"Well, you are doing an excellent job. Have I told you how amazing this date is? Because wow."

Bennett flushes even more than before as we dig into the picnic basket. He sets out our plates while I handle the thermos of lemonade.

"Everything is so cute! The sandwiches are hearts! I cannot believe how perfect this is!" I exclaim, patting Bennett on the leg as he hands me a baby blue plate holding a sandwich, strawberries and the cutest little pink cupcake.

He looks down and mumbles, "The hearts were my idea."

"They're my favorite! You are the very best!"

***

Bennett

My hands are full and I've never been happier. Betty keeps handing me things—the snow globes from earlier, a tiny spoon engraved with *Darlington*, and a birdhouse that looks like the train depot. She's still looking, admiring every silly little thing in this shop and showing them all to me.

"Look at these! Should I get pink or blue?" She chirps, holding up two shot glasses showcasing a train.

"Both," I say, taking the tiny glasses from her hands and adding to her stash.

"Should we get t-shirts? That could be cute, we can get a souvenir shirt everywhere we go! What do you think?" She asks, shimmying her shoulders.

I would wear souvenir shirts every day to see her smile.

"I would greatly enjoy collecting t-shirts with you."

She squeals and hugs me, almost making me drop her treasures, and I'm disappointed that I can't hug her back.

"Okay, so the big question is—matching or coordinating tees? Do you have a preference?" She digs through a rack of brightly colored shirts.

"Whichever would make you the happiest."

Please not the tie-dye.

"Let's coordinate because I really want this one, but don't think you'd enjoy wearing this." She holds up a *Darlington: The Most Darling Little Train Station* crop top, in hot pink, that would look ridiculous on me. A little more digging and she comes back with a black t-shirt with hot pink writing stating the same thing.

"I think those two are perfect." I breathe a sigh of relief that she didn't want us to wear tie-dye.

She tosses the shirts over her shoulder freeing her hands to touch more things.

"Oh! I've been needing a new water cup!" She exclaims, showing me a large, baby blue cup with the Darlington logo on it.

"That one is lovely, you should get the pink one too."

The smile she gives me is blinding. Nothing in my life has ever felt as good as her smile directed at me.

Maybe I can make this vivacious woman happy.

"Okay, okay. I'm done. I promise. I know you have got to be tired of lugging my junk around," she says, trying to take things from my arms, but I turn so she can't.

"I will never be tired of carrying anything that you want me to carry. If you have everything your heart desires, we can check out. But if you still want more—get everything you want."

She giggles, patting my arm. "Thank you. But I have enough to make my apartment Darlington-themed. I should leave some room for our future adventures."

Future adventures. She wants to go more places with me.

"I like that idea."

Love, I love that idea. And you.

***

Betty

"So, I might have caught myself a man," I say to the table, making my family pause mid-conversation and snap their eyes to me.

"Pigeon, what? Just... what," Danny's hand freezes, fork dangling midair.

"You aren't even divorced yet, right?" Dad asks, glancing at Mom. She gives him a little nod, confirming the technical status of my marriage.

"So, what's his name?" Mom snags a roll and breaks it apart to smear butter on it.

"Bennett Sterling."

"The billionaire?" Danny asks, his voice overlapping with my parents' similar questions.

"Yup," I answer them.

"That's the twerps boss!" Danny shouts over the commotion, waving his fork in the air.

"How did this happen, Betty Bunches?" Mom asks once everyone has settled down.

"Okay, so you know I've been taking myself on dates to mess with Trevor—"

"The twerp," Danny interrupts and Mom pops him on the shoulder.

"Anyways. I met him at the bar in L'albergo Verbania and we talked all night then we started going on friend dates." I take a bite of my mashed potatoes, wanting to enjoy my food before it gets cold. I should've waited to drop this bomb until I finished eating, but here we are.

"Friend dates?" Danny laughs. "Only you, Pigeon."

"Shut up. So, we do the friend dating and it is so much fun. Then I go to visit him at his office and Trevor—"

Danny interrupts to cough-say, "Twerp."

"Danny! Enough." Dad says, glaring at him.

I take a deep breath and exhale. "Trevor threw a punch at Bennett and got himself and his girlfriend fired!"

My mom claps. "That's the best news! Did your Bennett hit him back?"

"No! He didn't need to, just pushed Trevor against the wall. Everything went wild and Bennett moved me out of the way but then Bennett kissed me and now I have a boyfriend."

"Good for him, getting to handle that twerp. Damn good job, bring him around so I can shake his hand," Dad says, turning his attention back to dinner.

"Yes, sir," I tell him before my mom pats my hand.

"How was the kiss?" she asks, giggling.

"Ew." Danny gags.

Mom throws her napkin at his face, telling him to hush.

"But that isn't even all! He hired someone to track me down at my loft and Bennett, thank god that Bennett was there. What would I have done if he hadn't been?"

"Baby, maybe you need a restraining order if he's stalking you."

"Oh, Bennett had a security guy do something and now my house beeps every time I open a door. And I have a code. But, listen, Bennett practically threw him off of my porch. Off the porch! And—"

"What the hell?" Danny interrupts. "You've known this guy like a week and he gets to fight the twerp twice? You haven't even let me do it once!"

My eye twitches. "Because you're such a loser," I whine.

"Let her finish her story," Dad says, taking another bite of steak.

I sigh. "No, it's fine, I was done anyways. Just, I don't think Trevor is going to bother me again. Not after Bennett handed him his ass. Twice!"

Dad laughs. "I wish I could have seen that. Would've paid good money for it."

Sixteen

Bennett

I TUCK MY NOTEBOOK back into the bedside table. I'm in love with Betty. I knew I loved her on our date, but I'm actually *in love* with her. I want to spend every day with her and the thought of not being in her life makes my heart pound painfully. I want to touch her, hold her, breathe her air.

I would also like to have sex. With her. Only with her.

I'd always assumed that I didn't feel sexual attraction. I never had before. But with Betty, the connection was instantaneous—and the sexual desire followed soon after, really surprising me. It's as if, once I grew to know her personally, it unlocked all of these feelings.

And they are definitely unlocked.

I've spent the last couple of days processing this unexpected revelation. But what about Betty is expected? She tumbled into my life, bringing color and companionship, and I don't know what my life would be without her. She can't be ready to hear this. Her divorce hasn't even come through, and I'm ready to change her last name to Sterling.

"Bennett!" Stella yells through the house, the door slamming behind her. "You have a package!"

A ripple of excitement travels down my spine, similar to the feeling of finding a rare encyclopedia for my collection. That has to be Betty's purse. I rush into the kitchen, greeting Stella as I pass her. I open the box with a kitchen knife and pull out the embodiment of my feelings for Betty. I logged almost twenty hours of research to find this particular bag. Every moment was worth it.

It should be the exact shade of the shoes she wants to match, and I cannot wait to hear her squeal when she sees it.

"Find a new book for the collection? I'm going to have to get you a new bookshelf soon," Stella calls over her shoulder as she starts the dishwasher.

"No, no. Not this time," I reply absently. I finish unwrapping the bag and set it on the counter to admire.

"Wow." Stella whistles. "Chicky is going to love that."

"Do you think so? She wanted a bag to match a particular pair of shoes, so I found it for her. I hope."

"Let me see the shoes," Stella demands.

Opening my photo app, I show her the shoes and the bag styles Betty sent me.

"You did good, baby angel. She's going to wear a hole in that purse." Stella laughs.

"And that's good?" A hole in her bag sounds like a problem, not a positive.

"I mean, she is going to use that purse so much that it will eventually wear out. Because she's going to love it."

"Yes, yes. That is what I want."

***

Betty

"Oh, Bennett, it's so pretty in here!" I exclaim, taking in the candlelight and flowers. Bennett has set a beautiful table, dinner looks fantastic. It's straight out of a romance novel.

"Thank you. Stella cooked the meal, but I wouldn't let her help with anything else. I wanted to do this for you."

He is so precious.

I grab his tie and pull his lips down to meet mine, a quick brush.

"Thank you. It's perfect," I say against his mouth.

We pull apart, a small smile on his face.

"Would you like your gift before or after our meal, my dear?"

"You got me a gift!" I shriek, clapping my hands.

"I did. I think you will like it," Bennett says, giving me another kiss.

He walks deeper into the kitchen, opening the cabinet that Stella keeps glass baking dishes in, and pulls out a large hot pink gift bag. I follow him, too excited to stay where he left me, and make grabby hands for the bag. He chuckles—rusty and amazing—and hands it over.

I shove the crinkly tissue paper aside and gasp at the distinctive lime green box.

Is this... It can't be.

"Oh, Bennett, no. This is too much," I protest, lifting the lid reverently.

"Nothing is too much for you, my darling."

His words float over my head as I finally come face to face with the most perfect bag. A hot pink vintage 1963 Rosavento—a bag that I have admired my whole life but never thought I would own.

I own a Rosavento.

"Bennett. This costs more than my car—probably even my loft! How did you know?" I gasp, clutching the bag to my chest.

"You like it?" Bennett asks, a thread of doubt in his voice.

That uneasy tone stops my little dance. I look at him—his face anxious but pleased.

"This is the best gift I have ever been given. The best. But Benny-Boo, it's too much. You can't blow all your money on bags for me."

A wide grin lights his face—sunshine breaking through clouds. I'm mesmerized. I want Bennett to buy me more bags to see this smile again.

"My dear, I am not at risk of running out of money. Even if I was, it would be a privilege to spend my last dollar on you."

I fling myself into his arms, the bag smushed between us, and squeal. "Thank you so much! I'm going to change out purses right now!"

I rush over to my inferior purse and dump it on the counter, shimmying my shoulders as I move my sunglasses and wallet into my Rosavento.

Bennett bought me a Rosavento.

Bag change up complete, I look over at Bennett to see him watching me with a bright smile.

I would give up this bag to keep that look on his face.

***

I spare one last glance at my new purse, sitting on the counter where I could see it from the dinner table and let Bennett lead me into the living room.

"Would you like to have sex with me?" Bennett asks after settling me on his sofa.

"Yes. Now?" I wiggle in my seat.

He laughs, clearly relieved, and replies, "As much as I want to, I feel like we should finish this discussion first."

"Alright. I have the implant birth control and got tested when I decided to leave that asshole. So I'm good to go."

"Excellent. I've never done this before, so I haven't sought out testing. If you would like me to get tested, I will," he says.

"What do you mean? Never had a sex discussion before? Lots of one-night stands, huh?" I imagine sweet Bennett picking up women at a bar. But then the realization that he might've actually slept with those women makes the joke a lot less funny. Jealousy makes my heart pound before I notice Bennett's flushed face.

"I've never had sex before," he says after a long pause.

"Oh. Well, that is unexpected."

"Is it really?" he asks, still blushing.

Our kisses and his sexy smirk flash through my mind as I say, "Yeah, it is."

He laughs. "I was diagnosed with Autism at age three. Soon after my parents realized that forcing me to socialize wasn't working and they focused solely on training me to be an effective CEO. I went to an all-boys boarding school and then as an adult, I never felt the desire to go out with women. Until you. You, I desire. I crave you, darling."

"See? That right there! That's why it's hard to believe you've never done this before. You crave me? Whew," I say, fanning myself.

He gives me that sexy little smile. "Merely speaking the truth, dearest."

"Well, your truth is sexy."

"Shall we also discuss what we want or do not want regarding a sexual relationship?" he asks nervously.

"Yes!" I blurt out, shimmying my shoulders.

Bennett's face deepens in color as he pulls out a notebook that I don't recognize. His pocket notebook is a deep green, but this one is navy blue. He glances up at me but doesn't quite meet my eyes.

"So," he clears his throat and tugs at his collar. "Well, I, that is—"

I want to tell him to spit it out, but that might fluster him even more, so I take his hand and wait.

He takes a deep breath, squeezes my hand, and then opens the navy blue notebook. It's filled with his lovely handwriting. I barely restrain myself from reading whatever he wrote in there. I don't want to invade his privacy.

"I read every book that you wrote. They are wonderful, by the way. I made notations on the sex acts and figured out which ones you wrote about the most. I thought that if you wrote what you enjoyed or fantasized about, that perhaps this could be our *to-try* list."

Now it's my turn to blush. "I can't believe you read my books!"

He looks startled. "Should I not have?"

"Oh no! No, it's totally fine that you did! Good even. I just can't believe that you wanted to!" I assure him.

"I want to know everything about you. Of course, I have read your stories."

"If I didn't already want to sleep with you, I would now!" I laugh.

Bennett's face can't get any redder. He gives me that little smile and pushes the notebook in front of me, along with a box of miscellaneous writing utensils.

"Alright, I am going to highlight the ones that I want to do, and then we can go from there. Oh, wait. Did you only write down the ones that you want to do?"

"I wrote them all down. However, I think I would enjoy trying any of them with you," he says, still blushing.

"Okay, as long as you want to try them. I don't want you doing something just because I want to."

My face heats as I read through the list. He really did write down every single sexual thing in my books. I start highlighting. Turns out he was totally right that I put my fantasies in the books. I hadn't even realized that I was doing that.

When I finish, most of the page is bright yellow and I know that my face is as red as Bennett's. Imagining Bennett doing these things to me, with me, I might have to change my panties.

I slide the book back over to Bennett and say, "Okay, you underline the things you absolutely want to try, and we can go from there."

Without a moment's hesitation, Bennett proceeds to underline every single thing that I highlighted.

Yup, my panties are goners, for sure.

He glances up at me, face still red, with a sweet smile and asks, "Now that we have agreed on what we want to do, what about what you don't want? We should make a separate list."

He turns to a clean page and titles it *No,* and then writes down one line before sliding the book back over to me.

No degradation.

I look up at him, my head tilted to the side. He takes my hand and says, "I can't say mean things to you, even if they're sexy."

I smile, my heart in my throat. "Thank you."

He squeezes my hand before letting go. "Now, your turn."

"I don't think I have any absolutely nots. We might find some along the way but right now, I can't think of anything."

"Maybe we can schedule a relationship meeting once a month. We can discuss any issues and make changes to the lists. Or is that too business-like?"

"It does sound really business-y but I love the idea. How about the first Saturday of the month we do a date-night-in and use that time to talk about us?" I suggest.

"I'm adding that to my calendar right now. Should we create a shared calendar for our dates and important events?"

A rush of fluttering warmth spreads through my body. He says that so casually—no trepidation about combining our lives in this little way.

"Yes, I would like that very much," I say around the lump in my throat. I blink rapidly while he types on his phone. I don't want him to see me get misty-eyed over a damn scheduling app.

"Alright, you should receive a text to approve it," Bennett says as my phone dings with the notification.

"Got it, done! Awesome. Let's set up some more dates so our calendar isn't so empty!" I say, accepting our snazzy new shared calendar and admiring how he already has our monthly relationship meeting scheduled.

"Can I have all of your Saturdays? A regular date night would be perfect."

"Oh, yes, please!" I watch as a recurring date pops up on the calendar for the rest of the Saturdays.

"Would you also like to accompany me to the miscellaneous galas and work parties? I usually go alone, but now that I have you, I would like you to attend with me."

"Absolutely! Just toss those dates in and email me a list with the dress codes for these things and I'm there!"

"Will do, darling. Though I could have a designer send you outfits for these things. That is what my mother always did."

"Really? That sounds kind of fun, like being a movie star or something!"

"That is how you should always feel, though the first event we have is not for another eight months. But if you would like a designer to dress you for any reason, please let me know and we can make that happen whenever you'd like."

"Oh, I don't want to put you out. I'm sure I can find my own outfits for these things." I backtrack, not wanting to be greedy after he bought me a freaking *Rosavento.*

"Nonsense. If you want it, I want to give it to you. Nothing you desire will ever put me out. Unless I can not provide it, that would put me out greatly."

"Well, if you insist," I reply with an exaggerated wink. "I would love to be professionally dressed for your snazzy parties."

"If that is the case, I will always insist."

That is so hot. Speaking of...

"Now, about this sex thing. I think we should make it special, maybe get a room at L'albergo Verbania?"

"That sounds perfect. Tonight?" he asks, his voice eager.

"Yes, please!"

***

Betty

I can't stop giggling. We're in Bennett's car, his hand on my thigh, almost to the hotel.

He keeps shooting glances at me and blushing.

We haven't spoken since we ran out of his house, both too excited to talk.

Around the fountain and in front of the door, the valet takes the keys and I tug Bennett inside.

Lilith is at the reception desk. She smiles brightly as we approach. "Betty! Bennett, how are you this evening?"

"I'm well. Thank you for asking. How are you?" Bennett replies as I chirp, "Lils! I didn't know you were working tonight!"

"Wasn't supposed to, but we had a no-call, no-show and here I am." She rolls her eyes. "Here are your keys, do you need help with your bags?"

"Nope, we're good! I'll call you tomorrow!" I say, grabbing the key and Bennett's hand and dragging him to the elevator.

***

Bennett

Betty's enthusiasm is reassuring, even as I worry about how the rest of the night is going to go. Theoretically, I know what to do. I've read and reread Betty's books. But in practice, that's the root of my unease. But Betty is giggling and fumbling with the room key, and I know it will be great. I take the key from her and easily open the door, my arm around her. I do have our sex notebook—should we discuss how this is going to go? Or will that ruin the moment?

As soon as the door clicks shut Betty is pulling me toward her by my tie. My lips meet hers in a passionate kiss that throws all of my worries out the window.

I pull away to properly lock the door and flick on the light before letting Betty drag me to the bed. She pushes me gently until I sit on the edge. Straddling my lap, she slowly loosens my tie before slipping it over my head, kissing me the whole time. I run my tingling hands up and down her back, grabbing her bottom, pulling her tighter against me. She moans into my mouth—the most erotic sound ever created.

I feel the center of my universe shift. My sole purpose in this life is to make Betty sound like that forever.

My shirt is unbuttoned, and Betty is tugging it off.

I find the zipper of her dress and tug it down, sliding her dress off of her shoulders. She stands to drop it to the floor. I'm burning up—wanting to snatch her to me but also enjoying the view. Betty is clad in only a pair of yellow panties with tiny flowers on them and a white bra—an image that will forever be burned into my mind. Nothing has ever been this beautiful.

She is a goddess.

"You are gorgeous," I whisper reverently. She flushes and giggles, reaching her delicate hands behind her back to unsnap the bra. When her breasts are revealed, I know I'm in heaven. Did I think earlier that nothing could be as beautiful as Betty in a bra and panties? This. This is better.

"Can I slide your panties off?" I ask, reaching for her. She steps into my waiting hands, allowing me to tug her panties down her thick thighs, revealing her vulva.

"What do you want me to call it? Your vulva?" I murmur in awe.

"Pussy is always a fan favorite," she jokes, dropping to her knees to unbuckle my pants.

Once my penis is exposed, she whispers, "And this throbbing thing is your cock."

She then does the most magnificent thing and swallows my whole... cock. I've never felt anything like this before, all warmth and wetness. I pull her hair back with my hand to see myself disappearing into her mouth. I groan, unable to do anything but watch. Heart pounding, I tug her hair gently, pulling her head up so I can ravage her mouth. And ravage I do—I'm feral for a taste of her.

I slide my hands down from her face to her soft shoulders before tentatively touching her breasts. More than a handful, they're heavy in my hands. I softly rub my thumbs over her nipples, feeling them quickly turn into pebbles. She pants in my mouth, and I swallow the sound, needing more of her. I pull away and tug her to her feet. My pants drop to the ground. I kick them and my shoes off quickly.

"On the bed," I demand, watching her eyes dilate at the sound. *She likes me in charge.*

As I watch her clamber on the bed, I recall all of the sex scenes I've read, how the men behave. They growl and command, and they get to touch and taste her everywhere. That's what I want—my mouth on every single inch of this woman. I think she wants it, too.

My Betty gets what she wants.

I follow her onto the bed, running my fingertips up her smooth legs, marveling at the goosebumps that follow my hands. I continue my gentle path, skin to skin—up her legs, over her hips, her soft stomach, and around her nipples.

"Kiss me," she whispers, words that float through my soul.

I press my hard body to her soft one, kissing her like she's the prayer I never knew I was whispering.

I leave her lips to trail kisses across her face and down her neck. I gently nip and lick her nipples, reveling in her sounds. I stay here, tasting, tugging, kissing until her hips are restless under my stomach. I work my way down to her glistening feminine depths, mesmerized.

Every page I read, studied, disappears when my tongue touches her vulva for the first time.

I groan, spreading her thighs with my hands, and I feast.

Nothing has ever been better than this. Her body trembling, panting, moaning, her pink-tipped nails gripping the bedsheets. I stay where I am, sucking, licking, nipping until she tenses up and shakes, my name on her lips. I gentle my tongue, my hands full of her delectable bottom, and slowly lick her until the tremors stop.

I intend to do that again and again, but Betty moans, "Bennett, please."

My Betty begs for nothing.

I kiss my way up her body, touching and tasting her cotton candy skin. When I reach her mouth, she gently grasps my hard cock, notching it at her entrance. I slowly sink into her, fireworks behind my eyes.

I would sell all of my businesses and give away every dollar in my bank account to stay right here forever. I slowly move, watching her beautiful face, listening to her moans and gasps, following her lead. When her hips meet mine harder, I give her what she wants. More. Harder. Betty's sounds get louder, wailing, she drags her nails down my back. My hips piston into her, harsher. The base of my spine tingles, and I reach between our bodies to rub her clit in circles. Her cries get louder as she comes, trembling beneath me, pulling my orgasm from my body.

Heaven.

***

Betty

This man has ruined me.

I thank the stars above that he's mine.

I never knew sex could be like that. Passionate and gentle. Rough but loving. Perfect. And two orgasms? Let me die right now smiling.

Bennett is still inside of me—we're both trembling.

I'm in love with him.

My body aches in the sweetest way. He slips out of me, kisses my lips, once, twice, and says, "Let me get you a cloth."

Naked, he makes his way to the restroom. I hear the faucet turn on, then he is back, gently cleaning me up.

I cannot believe this is my life.

He gives me a sexy little smile as he crawls back up to gather me in his arms. He whispers, "Are you alright, darling?"

I can't help but giggle. "God, yes. Bennett..." I trail off, unsure if now is the right time to tell him that I'm in love with him.

He squeezes me to him, not rushing me, letting me gather my thoughts.

"I didn't know it could be like that," I breathe, tears stinging my eyes.

"It felt like I became whole for the first time in my life."

"Yes! Exactly!"

***

I awaken slowly—warm and safe, wrapped in Bennett's arms. I nuzzle my face into his chest, amazed that I have him naked in my favorite hotel.

"Are you awake, dearest?" he mumbles, voice thick with sleep.

I make a noise in affirmation, sliding my hand up and down his chest.

His hand finds mine, entwining our fingers—he brings my hand to his lips.

Butterflies erupt in my stomach, my heart roars in my ears.

Yup. I'm in love.

On the tip of my tongue, I almost blurt it out.

But then Bennett runs his fingers down my back. "Shall we take a shower, get ourselves cleaned up?"

"Maybe we can get a little dirty in the shower before we clean up." I giggle, loving this mood shift.

Bennett quickly rolls me onto my back, his fire-filled hazel eyes burning into mine. "Really? In the shower?"

"If you want to..." I say, feeling shy.

"I do. This wasn't in your books, though. We didn't add shower sex to the *to-try* list."

"I think it's okay to deviate from the list just a little and add it afterward."

His breathing ragged, he jumps out of bed and rushes into the bathroom, turning on the shower. He strides back into the room, his eyes feral and focused on me. I sit up and then I'm in his arms and his mouth is on mine.

He pulls back. "I would like very much to give you another orgasm. With my mouth. In the shower. May I?"

"Oh my god, yes." I moan, letting him sweep me away.

Seventeen

Betty

"Good to meet you, man. I'm downright jealous that you got to punch that twerp in the face. I've been wanting to do that for years, but Betty wouldn't let me," Danny says by way of greeting upon meeting Bennett.

We've barely sat down in my parents' living room. I love this room—it hasn't changed since I was a child except for new family photos. My mom is big on photos, professional or candid—she frames them all. Every surface is covered in frames: everything from Danny's Little League to me in my wedding dress. Mom replaced all the photos with Trevor the minute I said I was done with him.

The decor is very 90s sitcom—comfy and cozy, with a beige floral sofa, two matching armchairs, and a wood coffee table covered in magazines. A display cabinet sits in the corner, full of my great-grandmother's china, and a large potted plant sits by the door.

"Now, son, we usually wait until after dinner to talk about these sorts of things, but I am curious. How did it feel to take down the twerp?" my dad inquires.

Bennett's face flushes as he searches for a reply. "I didn't actually take him down, but it felt really good to silence him."

"Oh, tomato, potato, whatever. You got to hit the little twerp," Dad says.

"I'm sorry, Bennett. You have to excuse my bloodthirsty family—they were obviously raised by feral wolves."

Bennett chuckles, placing his hand on my knee. "I quite like it."

"See, Pigeon, he likes us!" Danny laughs.

"Oh, shush, he's just being polite."

Bennett startles and says, "No, no, that isn't true. I—"

Dad interrupts him. "Don't mind those two. Whenever they're at home, they become kids again and bug the shit out of each other and everyone else."

He relaxes and grins. "Yes, I can see that now."

"You're supposed to defend me!"

"Pardon me, darling. Yes, Betty is the epitome of maturity and all that goes with it," Bennett replies, a real smile on his face.

Guffawing, Dad claps Bennett on the back. "Exactly right there, son."

Watching Bennett gain the approval so quickly of my dad and brother causes a pang in my chest. *I almost missed this.* Why on earth did I think that my husband and my family not getting along was fine?

Mom pokes her head out of the kitchen. "You all come on. Lunch is ready."

I grab Bennett's hand, leading him to the kitchen table. My mom's kitchen is cow-themed. Why cows? Because when she was twenty and getting married she joked that she should do the kitchen in cows. Her friends thought that was hilarious and her entire wedding shower was nothing but cow stuff. Cow towels, cow clock, cow wallpaper border, cow curtains over the sink. Even the downstairs bathroom is cow-themed.

Momma isn't one for decorating. She says she already did it once—why worry with it again?

Plus, cows are funny.

My parents turn the conversation to Bennett's personal life as we sit at the table with fried chicken, potatoes, and Cajun rice on our cow plates.

"Pigeon told us that you've owned the Sterling Corporation for quite some time. You're awfully young for that, aren't you?" Dad inquires.

"I'm forty-three, so perhaps not very young. However, my father passed the reins to me when I was twenty-eight. I was raised to take over the company."

"Raised to take over the company? What does that even mean?" Danny interjects.

"Exactly as it sounds. From the time I could talk, I was trained to take over the company. My schools, social training, and extracurricular activities were chosen for that purpose."

"That's wild. Did you like it?" Danny asks.

Bennett looks contemplative. "Like or dislike never occurred to me. Until Betty, the very idea of doing things simply for enjoyment was a foreign concept."

"That's so sad," Mom says, looking like she wants to rush around the table to hug Bennett.

I look at Bennett, so composed even with my family prying into the heavy stuff over baked potatoes. I reach under the table and take Bennett's hand, giving it a couple squeezes. He gives me a small smile that lets me know that my family isn't scaring him away.

"Don't feel sad for me. While I am starting to believe that I missed out on a great many things, at the time, I didn't feel like I was missing anything."

"That somehow makes it worse," Mom replies, earning her a kick under the table from me.

"Well, that's okay," Mom continues. "Betty can drag you around until you get that childhood that you missed."

"That she can," Bennett responds, his cheeks flushed and a little smile on his face.

"When she takes you to Whimsy-World, I get to come, too!" Danny chimes in.

I blink rapidly, hoping no one notices that I've gone a little weepy. My family and Bennett, together, enjoying dinner. I finally feel like I can breathe without bracing for the worst.

I'm happy.

***

Betty

I'm sitting cross-legged on Bennett's bed, browsing the streaming services for a movie to watch, when Bennett walks out of his bathroom—black pajama pants and no shirt, chiseled chest on display. I know my interest has been noticed when I see him blush and give me that little smile.

He sits on his side of the bed, pulls out two black leather journals, and says, "I need to update my notebooks, then we can watch the movie."

I scoot next to him with interest. "What do you mean, update your notebooks?"

"Well, I have my pocket notebook where you've seen that I write down anything I want to remember or think about later. Then I have these bedside notebooks. One is where I keep track of the likes and dislikes of my acquaintances. The other is where I write down things to research or think about. I can contemplate and research when I have spare time—usually at bedtime. After spending the evening with your family I have quite a bit to update."

"Oh, I just love that," I reply, sitting back and watching him focus on his journals.

"Can I see my spot in your likes and dislikes notebook?" I ask excitedly, after waiting almost patiently while he makes his notes.

Curiosity eats at me as I wonder what he thought important enough about my preferences.

"You aren't in it," he says, not looking up from his notebooks.

Chest tight, my eyes burn. I thought I was important to him—shouldn't he make space for me? I take a shaky breath, this is fine.

He closes the notebooks and places them back in the drawer before pulling out a glittery hot pink notebook.

"This one is yours. After our first friend date, I knew you needed your own notebook," he says, handing me the cute journal.

My eyes fill with tears as I flip through. He has everything I've ever told him—from my ice cream preferences to my shoe size. I toss the journal on the bed and fling myself in his arms.

"Why are you crying, darling?" he asks, concern lacing his voice.

"You are so wonderful," I blubber.

"But why is that making you cry?"

"I thought you didn't care enough about me to include me in your notebook but then you had a whole notebook just for me."

Bennett squeezes me to him and rubs my back as he says, "My dear, I am in love with you. I know that we haven't been together long and if you don't feel the same way—"

I interrupt him with a squeal and pepper kisses all over his precious face.

"I love you, I love you, I love you," I say between pecks until he cups my cheeks, smiling, and gives me a toe-curling kiss.

Pulling back, I ask, "Can I write something in your Betty book?"

He looks at me seriously. "Darling, you can write in any of my notebooks. They are always available for your perusal or notes."

With a squeal I flip open the brightly colored pad and write on the next available page: *Betty is in love with Bennett.* Then I doodle some hearts and kissy lips for good measure.

Bennett looks at the new addition, his face flushed, and gives me the most brilliant smile ever. He takes the notebook from my hand and writes down something on the same page as my note.

Bennett is going to love Betty until the moment he dies.

"That's so morbid." I sniffle, then laugh. "And so, so sweet."

Eighteen

Bennett

HANGING UP THE PHONE, Betty's laughter floating in from the other room, I pull out my pocket notebook to write out the feelings weighing me down. Flipping through to find the next blank page, a flash of pink stops me. It's a post-it note. Heart pounding in my throat, I read and reread the note from Betty.

You make my heart happy.

I'm dizzy with affection for this woman—it's overwhelming. I want to touch her, breathe her air, but I restrain myself.

Placing the love note back where it was, I find a blank page and write my newest problem.

Work never felt like a burden until Betty crashed into my life. Before Betty, I never minded taking a call at any time. Now, it's intolerable. Nothing should ever pull focus from Betty.

The entire center of my world shifted when my lips touched hers.

Finished with my task, I flip back to the sticky note and read it one more time before tucking it into my desk drawer. I have a few other notes that Betty has written me in there, too. I love being able to read her letters whenever I want.

I pull out my phone and open the camera app before following the sound of Betty's laughter, trying not to let her hear me. I peer around the corner, finding her lying on my sofa with Yogurt curled on her chest, giggling at her phone.

She's so beautiful that I forget how to breathe for a moment.

I snap the picture before walking into the living room.

"Bennett!" Betty shrieks. "Come watch this video! It's a big dog scared of a kitten!"

Obliging her, I drop to my knees next to the couch. She smiles at me before pressing play. I chuckle, more amused by her than the animals.

"Finished your work?"

"I did, dearest. I'm sorry that I had to leave you on your own."

"No apologies! I know I'm dating a big shot," she says, winking. "Gotta do what you gotta do, and all that jazz. I don't mind hanging out with Yogurt while you do your thing."

"Thank you," I say simply, knowing that no amount of thanks will ever express how grateful I am for her.

But I will spend my life showing her.

She leans over, kissing my cheek, and replies, "You're welcome. Come sit with us!"

Betty holds Yogurt to her chest as she sits up enough for me to sit down, her head in my lap. I run my fingers through her hair as she soothes Yogurt, who did not appreciate being jostled.

She sighs happily. "That feels so good."

I smile down at her, so filled with bliss that my heart might explode.

"Want to spend the night at my place tonight?" Betty yawns.

My heart is definitely going to explode.

"I would love to. Does that invitation include Yogurt? I would worry about leaving her alone for too long."

"Of course I want Yogurt to come, too!"

How do I transport a kitten? She came home from the shelter in a cardboard box that I immediately discarded.

"I don't have a carrier," I state.

"Let's go to Pet-World!" Betty exclaims, dislodging Yogurt in her excitement.

***

Betty and I are standing in front of a massive selection of small animal carriers. The sheer amount available makes me want to run away. It's only Betty's hand in mine that keeps me grounded.

She points to a deep green one with gold accents and says, "Oh! That one looks like you!"

It would coordinate with my house. But I don't want that one.

I want one that feels like Betty.

"Which one would *you* want?" I ask, drawn to the pink and blue ones. Carriers with bows and bells, shiny things.

"You can't get one that I like! You're the one carting Yogurt around!"

"I will only use it to visit you and I would like it to show that. I will enjoy people knowing that my girlfriend picked out the carrier."

Betty squeals and throws herself into my arms, kissing my cheek.

I don't need my notebook to identify this feeling—joy.

"Okay, let me see," Betty murmurs to herself, touching the brightly colored carriers. "This one is the wrong shade of pink, too neon, right?"

She doesn't seem to actually want a response, so I admire her while she pulls cat crates down, chatting with herself. The pale pink shorts she's wearing ride up a little in the back, showing off her dimpled thighs and a glimpse of her perfect butt cheeks. Becoming aroused in Pet-World is not something I would enjoy, so I snap my eyes up to her dark pink cropped sweater that molds perfectly to her large breasts.

It seems to be impossible to look at Betty without craving her naked skin against mine.

Then she spins around, her ribbon wrapped high ponytail bouncing, clutching a pink carrier with baby blue trim. Her face is luminescent with happiness, stealing my breath.

"Look at this one! It's perfect! Listen!" She chirps, shaking the carrier to a symphony of twinkling bells.

She is perfect.

***

Betty

"Have you ever done weed before?" I ask Bennett.

We're sitting on my snazzy new royal-blue velvet sofa with Yogurt curled up beside us. Bennett ordered it after I gushed about how 'almost right' a gray velvet couch was. Sometimes having a rich boyfriend really pays off. I considered turning it down but if he wants to spend his money on a new sofa for me, who am I to stop him? It looks wonderful with my deep purple rug and emerald throw pillows. I've always wanted to decorate my home in jewel tones, it's like living in a tiara or something.

"No. It never occurred to me to want to. Have you?"

"Nope, Trevor was a jerk the one time I mentioned it," I reply, rolling my eyes.

"Would you like to try it?" he asks, with no judgment, just curiosity.

"If I did, would you do it with me?"

He looks surprised. "I suppose. If you wanted me to."

"Oh, I wouldn't want you to do anything you didn't want to."

"Now that you have brought it up, I am curious. I enjoy a drink now and then, and I have read that cannabis is better for you than alcohol."

I really do adore this man. "Bizarre that all of the after school specials made it sound so scary."

"Very bizarre, dear. Would you like to visit the dispensary and give it a try tonight? We don't have other plans. Or is this more of a daydream?"

"If you're serious. Like, you will get high with me tonight kind of serious. I would love to do it tonight!" I chitter, wiggling with excitement.

"I'm always serious about making promises and offers to you, my dear," Bennett says, ducking his head to catch my eyes.

I lean over to kiss him. He is so freaking swoon-worthy. Warmth spreads through my chest and I sigh into the kiss. He sits back, that cute small smile on his face, and runs his hand across my cheek. "You are a dream come true, darling."

"Your dream is to get high with a plump redhead?"

"Only if that redhead is you," he says, kissing my nose.

I crawl into his lap, wrap my arms around him, and squeeze. Sometimes, I swear I cannot get close enough to this marvelous man. He chuckles into my neck, arms around me, and says, "Shall I do some research and find us a dispensary to visit?"

"For real, real? You don't feel obligated or anything, right?" I don't want him to do things he doesn't want to do to make me happy.

His arms tighten around me. "I want to experience things with you. I cannot imagine there is much I wouldn't want to do with you."

"If this were 1815, I would totally swoon right now. Okay, okay! Research, babycakes! Let's do this!"

He laughs, the sound wrapping around my heart, and arranges us so he can hold me and his phone.

"San Remo Holistics is the closest highly rated dispensary near us," Bennett says.

I leap off his lap, grab his hands, and drag him up. "Let's go!"

He chuckles and lets me pull him to his feet. "Do you want to change first, darling?"

I glance down at my fuzzy socks, leggings, and oversized sweater. "Nah, as long as you aren't embarrassed to take me out in my jammies."

"I am nothing but proud to have you on my arm, no matter what you are wearing."

"Thank you," I say, my eyes watering.

Sometimes it's so hard to believe that he loves me for me, that he doesn't want to change a thing about me.

"Oh, darling," he says, concerned, pulling me into his arms.

I sniffle and grin up at him, hoping to ease his worry.

"I'm okay. Sometimes you are just too perfect for words."

He huffs, squeezing me to him. "Not as perfect as you, my dearest."

***

Bennett

I assumed that cannabis dispensaries would be places where I would not be comfortable bringing my Betty. But this place looks like one of those popular shops where famous social media people hang out. It's not for me, but not unsafe.

Perhaps the Sterling Corporation should investigate cannabis. If the nice location and full parking lot are any indication, this appears to be quite profitable.

"You're thinking about work, aren't you?" Betty asks from beside me.

"I'm sorry, dearest. I didn't expect a cannabis dispensary to look this nice. It must be quite successful."

"I bet it is. Let's go research, yeah?" she asks.

"If I weren't already in love with you, I would have fallen right then."

She does a little shimmy in the car seat. "You love me, you want to kiss me, you want to grope my boo-tay." she sings, smiling at me.

I chuckle, leaning over to kiss her. "Yes, I do."

I help her out of the car and keep a hold of her dainty hand. Threading our fingers together, we walk to the security guard posted outside, checking IDs.

***

Betty

"I think we bought too much," I laugh at our little bag full of goodies.

"Oh, we did." Bennett chuckles. "But we have no idea of what we like. I thought a little experiment would be fun. We can make notes of what we like and dislike about each variety. How can we know if we like cannabis without trying all of the types?"

"Good thinking! We should have a separate little notebook just for our experiments. I think I have one in a box somewhere," I say, bouncing to my closet to poke around.

Bennett's cross-legged on my ruby bedspread, sorting our haul. He's in black athletic pants and a gray tee that hugs his chest.

"Alright, this one will have to do," I say, bouncing on the bed, disrupting Bennett's organized weed situation. After ripping out the first handful of pages, I hand him the old composition notebook.

"Alright, then, dearest love. What would you like to sample first?" Bennett gestures to our sorted stash.

"Why don't we go classic and smoke a joint?" I shimmy my shoulders as Bennett smiles at me.

"Sounds perfect. Shall we set a few dates on the calendar to try the rest of our cannabis?"

I pull out my phone while Bennett packs the rest of our cannabis delights in the bag. We chat about dates, and I enter them into our digital datebook.

Pot date nights planned, we get down to the business of getting high.

Or we stare at the pre-roll and pull up a video of how to smoke it correctly.

"Well, that looks easy enough. Ladies first?" Bennett asks.

"Okey-dokey," I light it up and inhale—and immediately start coughing, handing the joint to Bennett and waving away the smoke.

He waits for me to recover before taking a puff. He lasts for a few seconds before erupting in a coughing fit.

Grimacing at the smoke, we repeat the smoking and coughing routine a few times until I start to feel tingly and buzzed.

Bennett chuckles when we finish the herbal cigarette, putting it out in our snazzy new ashtray.

I crawl over and straddle him, kissing him and feeling him under me. He runs his hands up my sides, which I usually love, but tonight tickles. I'm foggy and giggly, falling away from him and pulling him next to me on the bed.

"We should watch a funny movie!" I exclaim, running my hands through his hair and down his back.

"I will get the snacks prepared while you handle the movie."

Bennett is a little unsteady on his feet, but totally hot as he rummages around my kitchen. I pop my favorite movie into the

DVD player. From the kitchen, Bennett calls, "Are we watching that movie with all those babies?"

That is the funniest thing I've ever heard. I can't answer him through the laughter, but I do manage to press play as he climbs next to me on the bed. Still giggling, I crawl into his lap and wiggle around until he groans, his hands tightening on my hips.

"If you keep moving like that, we won't get a chance to watch the movie," he whispers in my ear, sending a shiver down my spine.

"Maybe I don't want to watch the movie," I whisper back, grinding slowly.

"You're playing with fire, my darling," he murmurs, sliding his hands under my sweatshirt. He kneads my breasts—so good, but I want more. I need to feel his lips on mine. I lean forward, trying to turn around to straddle his lap but only managing to fall sideways. Bennett tilts his head to look at my face, a little smile on his.

"Are you alright?"

"So alright. I think we should try number fourteen."

He looks so perplexed that I erupt into a fit of giggles. I can tell he is trying hard not to join in so I reach over and tickle him, loving his loud booming laugh. He tugs me up, still chortling, to straddle his lap. The merriment dies down, replaced with foggy sensuality, as Bennett slowly strokes the side of my face.

"You are ethereal, my dear. Simply stunning. I can not believe that I get to love you."

"Bennett, I'm the lucky one."

"Nonsense. You have ripped open my dull life and shone a light into all the crevasses. You are my joy."

Overwhelmed, I do the only thing I can, I kiss him. Slowly, exploring. Bennett's hands on my ass, I find the bottom of his shirt and, breaking our kiss, I yank it over his head revealing his chiseled chest. His lips tilt in that sexy grin and I crash my mouth into his.

Heart-stopping.

Too soon, he pulls back and whispers, "What's number fourteen?"

It takes a moment for the question to register, then it sets me off giggling again.

"I don't know, but if it's on our list it's going to be fun!" I squeak.

"Would you like me to retrieve our notebook so we can see?"

"I'll get it!" I dive off of him and rush downstairs to where his overnight bag is sitting. I plunder around until I find the right notebook. Glancing up at him on my bed, looking like the cover of a romance novel, I flip open the notebook and start giggling again.

"It's sixty-nine!" I yell, flinging the book back and bouncing up the stairs.

"Sixty-nine?" He asks, thoughtful.

I feel the heat rising up my face. "Yeah, like, I suck your cock while you eat my pussy."

"Oh. Oh, yes. Let's do that," Bennett says, excitedly.

"Really? You want to?" I ask, unsure.

"I want to do all of the sex acts with you, darling. But I really would like to eat your... vulva, again."

"Pussy."

"I don't think I can say that aloud." He looks uncertain, but not uncomfortable. So I push a little farther.

"Say it, I think it'll be sexy."

That seems to snap something in him, his eyes light up and he growls, "Well, then. Why don't you show me your... pussy and let me have a snack."

"Damn. That was totally hot," I murmur as I yank my sweatshirt over my head, loving how Bennett's eyes dilate at the sight of my generous tits. Then I slowly roll down my leggings, taking my basic panties with them. I shimmy my hips, mesmerizing my man until he grabs me and tosses me onto the bed. I giggle but then I'm covered by him and nothing is funny any more. He starts slowly, gently, kissing my face and down my neck, the tops of my breasts and then my nipples. I'm consumed by this moment, my skin overly sensitive and tingly. I'm whimpering as he teases me, tip of his tongue, scrape of teeth, feels so good but I need more.

"More, please." I plead, breathless.

He lifts his head and looks me directly in the eyes. "You don't beg me for a thing. You tell me what you want and I give it to you. The world is yours if you desire it."

He drops his head back to my bosom, rougher this time, tugging, licking, nipping.

Holy fuck.

I'm soaking the front of his pants as I grind my clit against his hardness, needing even more but lost to this feeling. He slows his movements, gently breaking away to ask, "How would you like to handle my ejaculation? In your mouth like you write?"

"Why don't you put it in my pussy instead? Let's sixty-nine until we're so close we can't stand it and then we do number fifteen—doggy style."

He groans, biting his fist. "Yes, please. Let's do that."

He lifts me off his lap, standing up to shove off his pants. His cock juts straight out, pointing at me, so I quickly get my mouth on it, swallowing it down to the root. He yelps, shoving his hands in my hair. He thrusts in my mouth before removing himself completely and crawling on the bed.

"Come sit on my face, darling."

I try to turn myself where I can straddle him and still suck his dick, but he flips me the other way. Barely giving me time to grip the headboard before he pulls my pussy straight down on his mouth, there's no way he can breathe like this. But he's moaning like I've sent him straight to heaven, his hands on my ass, pulling me down even more. Every flick of his tongue has my legs shaking, I'm going to crush him.

Electricity zips through my body—I don't even stand a chance as the orgasm crashes over me.

***

Bennett

Heaven.

Betty, trembling and grinding on my face, is the most exquisite thing I have ever experienced. She's all around me—the only thing I can see, feel. My nerve endings are on fire, and every sensation is at top volume. I'm overwhelmed and never want it to end. She stiffens, tremors wracking her body as she comes. I keep going, wanting—needing—more. She whimpers and pulls away a little, so I slow my tongue and let her go. She climbs down my body to hover over my throbbing member. Slowly she lowers herself, legs shaking, and rides me with short jerky motions. I grab her bottom, helping her keep momentum, loving the view of her luscious breasts bouncing with every pump.

"Harder," she moans, tossing her head back.

I grip her hips tightly and hammer into her, reveling in her sounds—all for me.

She collapses forward, hands on my chest, and slows us way down. Her eyes catch mine as she seductively smirks and rolls her hips—once, twice—*oh my god*. I pinch her nipple with one hand and her clit with the other, causing her to whimper and grind down.

"Bennett, I'm, I—" She sobs out, body shaking with release.

I grab her hips and pound into her until I reach my own orgasm, jerking inside of her.

I pull her in for a slow kiss, exploring her mouth as if I'd never tasted it before.

Betty is soft in my arms, languid in her movements. I roll us to our sides, pulling out of her as I do.

My hand on her cheek, I say, "I love you."

She covers my hand with hers, eyes shining with emotion, and says it back to me. Heart full, I kiss her again and extract myself to retrieve a warm washcloth.

***

Betty

"Nice ass!" I call out to Bennett as he descends the stairs, naked, to go to the bathroom. He flashes me that small smile that I love so much.

When the bathroom door shuts, I dig through his pile of clothes to find his pocket notebook. I open it to a random blank page and scribble a little note for him to find later. *Betty loves Bennett more than cotton candy ice cream.*

When the bathroom door clicks open, I'm laying back in the bed, waiting for Bennett. He gently cleans between my legs, his eyes roaming my body.

After tossing the used cloth in the hamper, he folds himself into the space beside me on the bed, wrapping me in his arms.

"We should make a sex check list!" I say, patting his chest.

"Would you like to do that now?" Bennett asks, stroking my hair.

"No, this is too comfy," I reply, nuzzling into his chest. "But don't let me forget to write this down later."

"What, my dear?"

"All of it," I mumble, drifting off to sleep, happy.

Nineteen

Betty

"Wanna do movie night at the house tonight?"

"Oh, yes! Do you know if they'll be home?" I ask, putting my phone on speaker so I can finish my makeup while I talk to Danny.

"Yeah, Mom had to work this morning. They'll be home."

"Nice, I haven't seen them in like two weeks." I laugh.

"Yeah, too busy with Benny-Boo-Boo to see your family."

"Oh, shut up, goose," I say, tapping my eyelid with a bit of shimmer.

"You first, Pigeon. Anyways. Is Bennett coming with you tonight?"

"Well, no, I didn't know he was invited."

"Of course he is, it's family time."

"But you all didn't want Trevor there and—"

"Whoa," Danny interrupts. *"Don't put Bennett in the same category as that fucker. I don't give a shit how long you were married to the twerp—he was never family. Bennett, though, I don't care if you two never get married. He's family."*

My throat tightens. I blink rapidly, hoping not to ruin the mascara I just applied, and respond, "Oh."

"Stop that! No crying on movie night! Invite your boy and we'll even let him pick the movie."

"I cannot believe you just called Bennett a *boy*. He's like twenty years older than you, loser."

"Fine." Danny laughs. *"Bring your old man. Whatever."*

"Rude!"

***

Bennett

Lukas, who has been filling in as my assistant since I fired Paige, buzzes my office to tell me that Betty is here. I tell him that I'll be right out, my heartbeat quickening.

I see her before she sees me—laughing at something Lukas said. A shiver of jealousy travels up my spine, but Betty spots me, and her smile brightens as she says, "Bennett!" and dances over to me.

"To what do I owe this honor, my dear?" I ask, leading her into my office.

"Can't a gal come see her boyfriend without ulterior motives?" She giggles, shimmying her shoulders.

"Of course, darling, but you so rarely do," I reply, a smile taking over my face.

"Well, you usually leave around this time so I figured you wouldn't mind."

"I never mind you stopping by. You can sit on my lap while I work, if you'd like. I know I would enjoy that greatly."

She tugs my tie until my lips meet hers and says, "I don't think you'd get any work done."

"I would give up the whole company just to keep you on my lap," I retort, fully serious.

"Well, why am I not on your lap right now?"

Good question. Heart racing, I guide her to my chair and pull her into my lap. She laughs, laying her head on my shoulder. I kiss her head, the scent of cotton candy in the air.

"I think I would like my office to smell like cotton candy," I say, my lips in her hair.

"Out of all of the scents that I associate with you, cotton candy is not one of them."

"I want my office to smell like *you* not me."

"Oh my goodness!" Betty chirps, sitting up to look at me. "Seriously? What would the big businessmen think when they step into the biggest businessman's office and it smells like cotton candy?"

"I have never cared what others thought of me and I don't intend to start now. In fact, I would like to add some Betty elements to this space."

She bounces in my lap, clapping her hands and smiling so wide that it's almost blinding. "Like what?"

"You know I am not a decorator, dearest. I believe that I will hand you my credit card and enjoy what you come up with—if that is alright with you?"

"That sounds like so much fun!" She looks around, chewing on her delectable lip.

"My only request is that you incorporate photos of you. A lot of them, actually."

"Betty business chic, I dig it," she says. "Now, down to serious business. Tonight Danny and I are having movie night with my parents."

"Well, I am glad that you came to see me before. I shall miss you tonight."

"No, no! Do you want to come to movie night? Danny said that you can even pick the movie!"

Warmth races through my veins. "I thought that movie nights were just for the Miller family."

"They are! And you're part of the family. I've felt that way since our first friend date but it was Danny's idea to invite you. And I know he means it because he never gives up his turn to pick the movie." Betty shines as she speaks.

My lips turn up into a full smile. Being accepted into her family feels better than closing any business deal ever has.

"We should watch that mystery movie that you like so much," I reply, tucking a stray hair behind her lovely ear.

"Oh! Yes! But this is your pick, not mine!"

"You know I don't watch movies. I really did enjoy the movie and would not mind watching it again with your family."

Betty maneuvers herself until she has her phone in hand and starts typing. She laughs and looks up at me. "Danny is *not* a fan of whodunits because he gets so stressed trying to figure them out. Usually, he vetoes my mystery suggestions, but he can't because it's your pick!"

"Glad to be of service, my dear."

***

Betty

"No way! Pigeon, you can't just have him choose your favorite movies!"

"He chose it all on his own!"

"No the fuck he didn't. Benny? Be honest," Danny says, turning to Bennett as I laugh.

"I haven't seen many movies, primarily just the ones that Betty has introduced me to."

"Wait. Really? You just don't like movies, or what?" Danny asks, confused. Movies were a huge part of growing up in my family. We'd always had movie nights, and trips to Coslada Video Rental were a special Friday night treat. My dad's DVD collection is absolutely massive—taking up three bookshelves.

"I have enjoyed what I've seen. I just grew up in a household where leisure time was spent on useful endeavors. We didn't even own a television," Bennett replies.

"That's a bummer, dude. Alright. Why don't we use movie nights to show you the best movies and get you caught up on pop culture?" Danny asks over his shoulder, searching the movie shelves.

"Wouldn't that ruin your fun? I don't want you all to have to rewatch movies simply for my sake," Bennett says nervously.

"Oh, we love rewatching movies!" I exclaim, patting Bennett's arm. He looks down at me, still unsure, and I immediately reassure him. "We almost always watch movies that we've already seen. That's why we let each other veto movies. One time, Danny picked this stupid sports movie for his turn five times in a row! That was like three months of every other weekend watching that crap. Showing you the best of the best would be a lot of fun, if you want to commit to movie nights with us for the foreseeable future?"

Relief in his eyes, Bennett says, "I believe that I would enjoy that."

"Sorry, Benny, I'm taking my turn back so I can show you this!" Danny laughs, waving a DVD in the air.

"Okay, that's a good one!" I say, watching Bennett smile at Danny's exuberance.

This is what life was meant to be.

Once again, I'm struck by how wrong I was in my marriage, and how I pulled away from my family, a little. Trevor made me believe that creating our own family unit meant I needed separation from my parents and brother.

But really he was just an asshole.

***

Bennett

Betty and I are cuddled up in a recliner, her on my lap, as the credits roll. Her parents went to bed about twenty minutes ago, since they both have to work tomorrow. Danny, sprawled out on the sofa, chatters about the director and the after credits scene that we are waiting for. Movie night at the Millers is an interactive experience, with popcorn being thrown, and Betty and Danny keeping a constant stream of conversation going, telling me actors and pausing to discuss the scene we just watched.

"Okay, Benny, watch this!" Danny exclaims, gesturing to the TV.

Betty giggles against my neck and whispers, "Can you tell this is his favorite movie?"

I kiss her head in acknowledgment.

After the superheroes set up the next movie in a humorous way, Danny says, "Next week we can watch the next movie. There are about thirty of these, so we're set for a while!"

"Hey! No! I get to choose next time. We're going to alternate. We aren't spending the next year of movie nights rotting my boyfriend's brain." Betty complains, sitting up to glare at her brother.

"Fine. But you liked the movie, Bennett?" Danny asks.

"I did, greatly. It was very fun. I see why you enjoy it so much."

Betty and Danny are still bickering as we all head out of the door, with Betty locking it behind us.

"Bethany!" an unpleasantly familiar voice calls out from a car parked across the street.

"What's that fucking twerp doing here?" Danny growls, slamming his open car door shut.

"Will you allow me to handle this?" I ask Betty, hoping she'll agree to sit in the car.

She shrugs, exhaustion with this situation dimming her eyes. "Sure."

I help her into the car as Danny confronts Trevor, who is storming up the driveway.

"I need to talk to my wife," Trevor snaps as Danny stands chest to chest with him.

"You don't have a wife," Danny snarls, his body tense and ready for a fight.

"Danny, let me handle this," I say, hoping to avoid a physical confrontation.

Danny looks at me and takes a step back but doesn't relax.

"I know that I told you, twice, to leave Betty alone. Why are you here?" I say, carefully watching Trevor, who is looking horrible. His eyes are bloodshot, his clothes are rumpled and covered in bleach spots.

"I, uh, I. Why are *you* even here?" Trevor stammers, clearly not expecting to see me.

The thought that he wanted to accost Betty, in front of her parents' house, at almost midnight, makes fire burn throughout my body. I take a deep breath, calming my agitation, and try to decide what to do. This needs to end. I cannot have this hanging over Betty's head any longer.

"Why are you here?!" Trevor shouts.

I doubt my ability to hold myself back and keep calm. I clench my fist, craving the crunch of his nose.

The car door creaks open and Betty's soft footsteps fall behind me. I unclench my fist and reach my hand back to take hers, offering her support if she wishes to confront her ex-husband. Her touch does more to calm me down than anything else ever could.

"What do you want, Trevor?" Betty asks sadly.

"You! I want my wife back. I'm so sorry about everything. Please, give us another chance. I don't care that you fucked him. I just want you."

Betty squeezes my hand and sighs. "You don't want me, Trevor. You never really did. Go marry Paige, or someone like her and move the fuck on. I'm tired. I'm tired of all of this. Please. Please just leave me alone."

I pull her firmly into my arms, shattered by the defeat in her voice. My rage is bubbling—no one makes my Betty feel this way.

"Betty, please. We were happy once, please."

"Betty has asked you to leave her alone. Leave before we get law enforcement involved. And do not bother her ever again."

"Fine. Betty, you're throwing our marriage away for nothing. Don't come crawling back to me when he finishes with you."

"That is enough!" I bark as Danny lunges forward. I'm able to grab his collar before he touches Trevor. Danny glares at me, grumbling about never getting a chance to lay the bastard out. Stepping around Betty, fist clenched, I wait to see what he does next. His eyes drop to my hand and his face pales. Trevor trips over himself as he runs back to his car, landing on his back in the middle of the street.

Betty's laugh twinkles around us, interrupting Danny's loud guffaw. We watch Trevor scramble up and fling himself into his car, tires screeching as he flies out of the neighborhood.

I turn to Betty, weariness clear on her face. She steps into my waiting arms, where she belongs, and mumbles against my chest, "Why won't he leave me alone?"

Danny bounces over to us. "Did y'all see that shit? Twerp fucking busted his ass getting away from us!"

Betty looks at him. "If he shows up again, *I'm* going to punch him. I'm so done."

"Hell yeah!" Danny cheers, patting his pockets. "I can't find my keys."

Betty looks up at me, a small smile on her lovely face. She shakes her head, and tugs my collar until my lips meet hers.

"Got them!" Danny exclaims from behind us, keys jingling. "Gross, you two!"

Betty pulls away, giggling, telling Danny, "Shut up!"

"You first!"

I cannot believe that Betty's ex-husband showed up, caused a scene and here I am—laughing.

Twenty

Betty

"Happy nine-month relationship meeting!" I laugh, throwing myself into Bennett's arms the moment he opens the door.

I get that small smile and a kiss on the forehead. "Happy nine-month relationship meeting to you, too, my dear."

His dining room table is covered in a white tablecloth with fancy dishes and pink flowers decorating the space. He always goes all out for our relationship meetings, making them magical experiences where we eat the best food while having open and honest conversations about our wants and needs.

"It's so pretty!" I exclaim, touching the flowers.

"Not as pretty as you," Bennett says, helping me into my seat.

Practically swooning, I'm left speechless. I can't believe this is my life.

Bennett dishes up my plate and his own, sitting beside me at the table so he can hold my hand.

"Betty, would you like to discuss taking the next step in our relationship, or would you prefer to stay as we are for now? I know that your divorce just came through. I don't want to pressure you."

My heart races as I answer. "My divorce has nothing to do with us. I am absolutely ready to hold your hand and take however many steps you want to take."

"Well, my dear, I would like to marry you. However, I understand if it might be too early—"

I interrupt him with a shriek and launch myself into his lap, silencing his lips with my own.

"Of course I want to marry you!" I say, planting kisses all over his sweet face.

Bennett lets out one of his rare laughs, hugging me tightly to him. He kisses my forehead and says, "Would you like a public or private proposal?"

"This wasn't the proposal?"

"Of course not. You deserve better than a kitchen table discussion."

"But we have candles and a nice dinner. That's all pretty romantic." I look around the dimly lit dining room.

"I'm glad you think so. Nevertheless, I would like to propose in a manner that you deserve. Would you like your family there, or just a private moment between us, followed by a dinner to announce it to your family?"

"I think I'd like it to be private and have a little party afterwards."

"Perfect."

I shimmy my shoulders a bit. "So, when are we getting engaged?"

"Patience, darling. I want this to be perfect for you. Now, we do have one final thing to discuss."

"After the getting-married discussion? What could we possibly have to talk about after that?" I ask, leaning back to look at his face.

He gives me that little grin. "Along with marriage comes combining our two households. Would you like to wait until we are married to move in together, or do that prior to the wedding?"

"Oh," I say, thoughts racing.

"Oh?" Bennett asks, concern apparent on his face.

"Yeah, where would we live? I don't want to live in Coslada, but your office is here. I don't want you to have such a long commute, either."

"I was already planning on buying a house in Verbania to be closer to you. We could pick one out together. Unless you don't want to give up your loft?"

"Were you really? I would love to get a house with you! I mean, yeah, I love my loft, but I would much rather have a house with you!"

"Wonderful, darling. I plan on working from home most days so I won't have a long commute. I will have to go in for meetings and other unavoidable things. However, those will only be once or twice a week."

I pat his chest excitedly. "Bennett! We're going to live together!"

"Yes, we are, my dearest love. And get married," he answers, giving me a blinding grin of his.

I let out a giddy squeak and kiss him all over his handsome face.

***

Bennett

"I've got a big question for you. Do we wear our Darlington shirts, or is that too cheesy?"

My heart races as I wipe my damp palms on my trousers. I want to surprise her with a proposal where we had our first date but I know she would hate wearing a silly T-shirt in the engagement photos. I hired a stealthy photographer to document the whole date from afar. I don't like being even a little dishonest with Betty, but is this really a lie? The thought of her little excited dance steels my resolve to keep this a surprise.

"I thought it would be nice to dress up, but whichever you prefer is perfect to me." *Please want to dress up.*

"It would be nice to get all fancy. Alright, you wear a nice suit and I have the perfect dress! It's baby blue if you want to coordinate your tie to it."

"Thank you, darling. I have the perfect tie," I say into the phone as I slump onto my couch.

"This is going to be so much fun. I'm going to get off the phone so I can get ready. See you at one?"

"Of course. I cannot wait."

"I love you!" She chirps.

"I love you, too."

I set my phone on the arm of the sofa with shaking hands. I sink farther into the couch as I close my eyes and try to calm my pounding heart.

"Why are you so nervous? You know she's going to say yes," Stella says, stomping into the living room.

"I just want this to be perfect for her."

"Chicky's gonna think this is perfect regardless. Don't stress yourself out. You know she wouldn't want you feeling like this over y'all's engagement."

"I know. But she deserves perfect," I say, getting up to pace the floor. Anxious energy radiates over my skin.

"Fuck, son. You need to take your ass to the gym so Betty doesn't see you this way and think something's wrong."

"You're right. I don't want her to worry. Not today."

I slide my feet into my athletic shoes by the door and run to the gym. Outside of Betty, this is my favorite place—not this gym in particular, but any gym. I marvel that this used to be my only version of joy. A pleasure allowed to me by my uninterested parents. Now my world is an explosion of giggles and elation.

I start my warm up and let everything fade away into counting repetitions and feeling my muscles burn.

***

Betty

Bennett is proposing today. I thought he might be when he didn't immediately agree to wear our Darlington shirts. The man bends over backwards to do what I want. He keeps patting his suit pocket and wiping his hands on his pants.

Not that I'm much better—my stomach flutters every time his hand brushes that pocket. I have to bite my lip to stop myself from smiling too hard—I don't want to ruin his surprise. He is so adorably nervous, and all I want is to wrap him in a hug and tell him *yes, yes, yes,* before he even has a chance to ask.

I love him so much.

He's so handsome today wearing a dove grey suit with a baby blue tie that perfectly matches my off-the-shoulder A-line dress. I went with a white belt, bag, and pumps. I wanted to look bridal but not *really*—I think I pulled it off.

The train car feels even more beautiful than it did the first time. Seeing it with Bennett's hand holding mine, knowing what he has in his pocket, makes it feel even more lush, more rich.

I'm going to marry this man.

We watch the scenery chug by, chatting about what we see. Silly stuff, both knowing that something big is right around the corner. The tension is palpable—I really hope Bennett can't tell that I already know.

The train slows to a stop, and we are back in the magical wonderland of our first date. My hand in Bennett's, the picnic basket over his arm, the sun on our faces while the scent of honeysuckle welcomes us—the same as last time, but different. More special.

I'm going to remember this moment forever.

Bennett arranges the blanket by the stream with shaking hands. When he has the picnic basket just so, he pops it open and rummages through it. While he sets up the blanket, I take a moment to immerse myself in this moment, one of the most meaningful days of my life. I close my eyes and lift my face to the sun, the gentle rustle of Bennett's movements and the stream surrounding me.

When I open my eyes, I see Bennett, drenched in sunlight and on one knee, displaying a ring.

"Betty, I—"

"Yes!" I squeal, tackling him to the ground. I kiss his eyes, cheeks, ear, whatever I can get my mouth on while his soft laughter wraps around me. He tightens his arms and rolls us until we are on our sides.

Nose to nose, he smiles the most beautiful smile and whispers, "Will you marry me, darling?"

My eyes fill with tears that I don't try to hide. "Yes, of course I will."

"Thank you," Bennett says, his eyes glowing.

"For what?"

"Loving me. I never imagined that I would feel this way—even more, that you would love me back."

"Bennett..." I say, too choked up to finish.

We stay like that for a long time, breathing each other's air, until a voice says from behind me, "Um, excuse me, sir?"

We both startle apart like naughty schoolchildren, faces red.

"The train is going to leave soon. Thought you guys might want to know." A sweet faced brunette with a camera around her neck, tells us.

"Thank you, Ms. Ventu, if you could take a few posed photos of us on the train, you can be finished for the day."

I look at him in surprise as Ms. Ventu thanks him and heads back to the train.

He really thought of everything.

"You hired a photographer?"

"Of course, I want these photos to wallpaper my office with."

I gasp, overcome with excitement. "Oh my god! Where did the ring go?"

Bennett pats his pocket before quickly looking around and finding the ring in the grass, dusts the box off, and pops the lid open.

Bennett takes my hand, presses a kiss on the palm, and slides the most beautiful ring that I have ever seen onto my hand. An emerald-cut sapphire surrounded by tiny diamonds glitters in the sun and its band is braided white gold.

It's perfect.

Our moment is interrupted—again—this time by the train conductor yelling about it being time to board. We are the only ones still out on a blanket, everyone else has already packed up.

Laughing, we rush to throw everything in the basket—except the most precious ring on earth, which will always be on my hand.

Twenty-One

Betty

WITH SO FEW EMPLOYEES, Enchanted Verbania's break room is always empty. Normally, I don't mind—I love having a moment to drink my coffee in peace—but today feels stifling.

I'm engaged! I'm barely divorced and engaged! I'm waiting on the panic to set in, but it hasn't. I worried that my family would think it's too soon, but all they did was celebrate.

A whisper of dread washes over me. *Is* this too soon? It's been just over a year since Trevor's betrayal, but it feels like a different lifetime. Heart pounding—why would I even want to get married again? *Did I get swept up?*

I picture Bennett's sweet face. It might be too soon. I might not be totally healed from my previous marriage. But I know that Bennett is the one that I want to wake up next to every morning. Marrying him feels like it was always meant to be.

I was meant to be right where I am.

Why should we wait? I did everything right with Trevor, dated for a year then engaged for another—he still betrayed me.

And Bennett would never do that.

As if to end my ruminating, Fable joins me at the little table, coffee cup in hand.

"Hey there, how'd your party go?" he asks.

And poof, every bit of doubt vanishes. The pure joy that washes over me at that question is proof enough that this is right. When I think of marrying Bennett all I feel is happy.

"So good! I hate that you couldn't be there, though."

"Someone had to be here, and I couldn't very well make you miss your own party just so I could go." He laughs.

"True that! Okay. I have news."

"Good news, I hope!"

"The best! We had the party to announce that Bennett and I... drum roll please!" I giggle, drumming on the table. "We're engaged!"

"Oh! That's wonderful! Congratulations!"

"Thank you!" I say with a wide smile, tapping my hands on the table.

"Probably going to be one of those huge, fancy shindigs, right? All high society and stuff."

I hadn't considered the actual wedding, I've only been thinking about marrying Bennett.

Shrugging, I reply, "I guess so. I haven't really thought about it."

Fable chuckles, leaning back in his chair to grab the coffee pot on the counter behind him. "I thought you ladies loved planning a wedding. Isn't that something little girls dream of?"

"Yeah, I've just been so wrapped up in getting engaged that the wedding hasn't crossed my mind."

"I'm sure you have plenty of time. Tell Bennett that I said congratulations. I've got to get back on the floor."

"Will do! I'm right behind you."

***

"Good morning, dearest," Bennett says, pulling me in for a kiss. We're standing on my porch, and he looks extra dapper in a dark gray suit with a pale blue shirt.

"Good morning." I sigh dreamily before giggling. "We match!"

I'm wearing a baby blue halter dress with a wide hot pink belt and matching wedges. My hair is piled on my head with a hot pink scarf wrapped around it.

"I should have worn a pink tie today," Bennett replies, taking my hand and walking me to the car.

"We'll have to plan better next time." I push up onto my toes for one more kiss before letting Bennett help me into the car.

"I have keys for four houses today. The realtor felt that these met our requirements the best. Would you like to have lunch with me afterwards?"

"Oh, yes! And you haven't seen these houses, right? You're going to be surprised with me?" I verify.

"Of course. I will always keep my promises to you," he says seriously, kissing the back of my hand.

"I know you will—I'm just so excited, I had to make sure!"

"I'm excited, too, darling."

I pull down the visor to swipe on some hot pink lip gloss. I never do my lips before Bennett picks me up—I like getting my kisses first. As I'm putting the gloss back in my bag, we pull into the driveway of an amazing house right across the road from the beach. It's painted pale pink with baby blue shutters, looks like the dollhouse of my dreams. I can imagine sitting on the front porch, drinking coffee, and watching the ocean.

"Oh, Benny, it's perfect." I sigh, clutching his arm as he helps me out of the car.

"It is pretty marvelous. Shall we see if the inside matches the outside?"

"I don't know. It's perfect, but what if the inside isn't? I don't want to know if the inside sucks."

He chuckles. "But what if it's perfect on the inside, too? What if this is our home?"

"Oh! Good point! Let's go see!" I drag him up the stairs to the perfect baby blue front door.

He lets us in, and I could cry. It really is perfect. Bright and airy, light wood and white. The kitchen, dining, and living areas are all one room with huge windows all around. The upstairs houses a huge sunroom that faces the ocean and three bedrooms.

I need that sunroom.

I'm so glad that it's only Bennett and me viewing this house because I cannot keep my cool. I am bouncing on my feet, touching windows and counters, and running from room to room.

"I need this house," I say to Bennett seriously.

"I agree that it is quite perfect. Would you like to see the others before we make the official decision, though?"

"I guess," I whine. "We really should look at them, at least. But I don't think any of them will be as perfect as this one."

"Perhaps not, but it will still be a fun adventure."

***

Bennett

Betty wiggles in her seat as she enjoys her sandwich. I adore that little shimmy she does every time she eats something delicious. Her vibrance and joy in life have altered me so greatly that I don't think I could survive without her light now.

"How is your lunch, my dear?"

She quickly swallows and taps her mouth with the paper napkin advertising *Coyote Cafe*, the delightful shop that we decided to have lunch in.

"It's so good, this might be the best sandwich I've ever had! How's yours?"

While Betty has a brie, apple, and fig jam sandwich, I went with my usual: turkey and cheese. "It is exactly as I expected it to be."

She laughs and pats my thigh under the table. "I'm so glad."

We finished touring the other houses and are very secure in our choice of house number one. I've never particularly cared what kind of house I lived in, as long as I can conduct my business, have access to a gym, and get a good night's sleep, it's all the same to me. But my Betty—she loves house number one, and that makes it perfect.

My phone rings, and seeing that it is our realtor, I excuse myself from Betty and walk outside to take it. The owners of the pink house immediately accepted our offer, and the agent wants us to come in and get the paperwork started.

"Well, my dearest, looks like we have a house," I say, sitting down.

Betty lets out the cutest squeak and rushes around the table to sit on my lap and sprinkle kisses all over my face. I'm laughing, and we're causing a scene.

The waitress comes by with a big smile and a slice of cake. "Looks like we're celebrating!"

Betty looks up at her, eyes shining, so beautiful I can't catch my breath. "We just got my dream house!"

"Oh! Congratulations! That is so exciting!" She sets the cake on our table.

Waitress gone and Betty back in her seat, I say, "We need to go by the realtor's office and start on the paperwork. We have quite a few things to do before we can start moving in."

"Boring!" Betty chirps, pouting with amusement in her eyes.

"But still necessary, my love."

***

Betty

"Well, Betty-Bunches-Of-Oats, I think we've gotten you all moved out," my mom says, looking around my empty loft.

I haven't lived here long, but it was my sanctuary after leaving Trevor and beginning my life with Bennett. Now it feels like a chapter fully closed. No more limbo. I've found my forever home—and it's even more wonderful than I ever imagined.

"Thanks for the help," I gather the last of our cleaning supplies into a bucket. Bennett, Danny, and my dad are at the new house, unloading my furniture. I thought Dad was going to lose his mind when Bennett offered to hire someone to move me. Turns out, *'Millers can do it all on their own'* is apparently a family motto—one I've somehow never heard until today.

So now my gazillionaire fiancé is hauling furniture like he wasn't signing million-dollar contracts yesterday.

"Let's grab the boys some lunch before we head to your house," Mom says, taking the bucket from me so I can get my key off of my keyring. After chipping two nails, I manage to swirl the dang thing free. I place it on the counter, snap a selfie with the key, and send it to Bennett.

We officially live together!!!!!

I add a bunch of heart and kissy-face emojis and press send, with my mom rolling her eyes.

"Alright, let's do it to it!" I say, dancing out of the front door for the last time.

***

Betty

All of our things are in our new home. Boxed up, sure—but here. Together. My family left, and now it's just us in this bare house filled with our mismatched furniture. We decided to keep all of our combined pieces for now, see what we like in the new space and what should be donated. Or what Danny wants—he always gets first pick before furniture hits the donation pile.

"Darling, shall we begin unpacking the boxes or wait until tomorrow?"

"Let's go ahead and do a couple. Our dinner won't be delivered for another hour, I think." I sit on the floor in front of one of Bennett's many bookcases and flip the lid of a box of books. "You have a preference on how these are shelved?"

"I do. However, with the addition of your books and bookshelves, I will have to rethink my whole organizational method to include yours. So for now, we'll just make everything look nice—and later I will sort it properly."

"Aw, we're going to combine books?" I slide a fancy leather-bound book on the shelf.

My silly romcoms are going to look hilarious next to his fancy tomes.

"I assumed so, darling. But would you rather not?" He asks, settling next to me on the floor.

"Oh no! I love the idea—my books all close and personal with yours. Just... yours are so snazzy and mine are not."

Laughing, I reach over his lap to pull out one of my books and slip it in between a couple of his.

He looks at the shelf contemplatively before shrugging. "I quite like it."

We work side by side, Yogurt occasionally popping in to climb on the shelves. Until I notice Bennett flush and stiffen. He sneakily tries to slide a scrapbook onto a bottom shelf.

I should let him keep his secret, but I'm definitely the kind of cat that curiosity killed.

"What's that?" I ask, a bit anxious about what he was trying to hide from me.

Bennett slowly pulls the photo album from the shelf, glances at me nervously before silently handing the baby blue book to me.

I shouldn't have asked.

"I'm sorry, you don't have to show me—you can have your secrets," I say, shoving the album back to him.

"My dear, to you I am an open book. I don't mind you seeing this. I just feel a little ridiculous."

I open the scrapbook and find notes I have written him—love letters tucked in his notebook, post-its with scribbled hearts left on his bathroom mirror, grocery receipts with *I love you* scrawled across the back.

He kept them all.

I should have known he would.

Bennett's precious face becomes blurry as tears fall down my cheeks. For a moment, all I can do is clutch the book and cry.

"Darling?" Bennett's voice sizzles with anxiety, snapping me out of my cry-fest.

"Bennett!" I squeal, throwing myself into his lap and knocking him flat on the floor. His strong arms wrap around me, holding me tight.

I lean back, rest my hands on his chest and look down at him—my heart bursting with affection.

"Thank you," I say simply, no other words forming.

He stares at me, searching, then smiles and says, "I love you."

"I love you, too. So much."

***

Betty

"Betty, darling, we have a problem."

I look up, startled, from the book I'm reading. "What's wrong?"

"I have a hyperfixation," Bennett says, pacing the room.

"Isn't that what autistic people do? Get hyperfixations? Aren't they fun? Why is it a problem?"

"Yes, very fun. But I am hyperfixated on your pussy." He rakes his hands through his hair, voice rough. "All I want to do is look at it, touch it, taste it, pleasure it. I can barely focus on my work."

Warmth spreads through my body as I watch my so-put-together partner lose his shit over my pussy.

Giggling, I stand up and reach under my poofy yellow skirt to slide off my thong. I toss it to him, and he snatches it out of the air, pressing it to his face, inhaling deeply.

Bennett shoves my panties into his suit pocket before hitting his knees right in front of me. He quickly tosses my skirt over his head and grabs my ass to pull my pussy right to his mouth.

The first swipe of his tongue makes me giggle—it tickles—but he grips me tighter, anchoring me to his mouth. And just like that, any thought of laughter is gone.

Twenty-Two

Betty

"Whatcha wanna be when you grow up?" Lilith asks, tossing a piece of popcorn in her mouth.

We're curled up with Yogurt on my daybed in the sunroom. Surrounded by windows, the sun setting over the ocean casts the room in a pink glow. A silly 90s romcom that we aren't watching plays on the little baby blue framed TV mounted on the wall by the door. I haven't fully decided on the decor in this room, but so far I have a ruffled pink lace bedspread and a chair that perfectly matches the ornate television frame.

I laugh. "I've been married, divorced, and almost married again. I think I'm already a grown up."

"Oh shush," she says, tossing a floral throw pillow at me. "You know what I mean. You gonna keep working at Enchanted or take up a charity cause or whatever it is that rich wives do."

"I'm definitely going to keep working, and since Bennett insists on paying for everything, I'm going to buy myself a bookshop."

"And compete with Fable?" Lilith asks, folding herself into a cross-legged position.

"Oh no! You know how small Fable's romance area is," I reply as Yogurt starts kneading my chest, purring. "So, I was talking to him the other day and he wants to expand the children's section eventually, but that would mean making big changes to what he stocks. Like, if he cuts the romance, I could open a romance-only bookshop. Especially if I can get a building in the town circle."

"That would be so stinking cute! Like sibling bookstores!"

"Right? Exactly! Poor Bennett is freaking out that I won't let him buy me a building and stuff, but I have to do this on my own, you know?""

"No, I don't know. If I had a bujillionaire I'd let him buy me everything!" Lilith chuckles.

"I did let him buy me a house," I say, gesturing around the room, accidentally jostling the kitten lying on me. Yogurt stretches and hops off me onto the hardwood floor with a soft thud. "But I really want this for my own. I need to do this on my own."

I sit up, tucking my legs under me, dusting the cat hair off my chest.

Lilith nods. "That's cool. Not for me, but really cool."

"You think I'm being ridiculous, don't you?" I ask, picking at a little lint ball on my sweater.

"What?" She gasps. "Not at all! I dig that about you, that you want to work for it. I'd fold like a cheap lawn chair, is all I meant."

"Really?" I ask, insecurity weaseling its way to the top of my emotions.

Lils rolls her eyes. "Duh. It's great. Building something just for yourself, especially after the bullshit with your ex, it's perfect for you. I'm just made to be taken care of, bummer that I don't have anyone to do that."

"Wanna find you a man, huh?" I say, wiggling my eyebrows.

"Nah, I'm not looking. If a hottie chases me and puts in the work, I might consider giving him a go. Maybe. Boys seem like a lot of work. I don't even know how often to feed one. Do they need a lot of exercise? I bet they even want to sleep in your bed." Lilith shudders dramatically.

I bark out a laugh. "Oh my god. If you find a good one they handle all that on their own. But yes, they do sleep in the bed."

"Ew. I like having the whole bed to myself. I wish I could find a man that would fuck me senseless, buy me shiny things, and then leave me alone to sleep."

"Like a roommate with benefits?" I ask, still chuckling.

"Yes! Exactly! All the good stuff and then separate beds."

"That kind of bums me out, I love cuddling."

"Yeah, I absolutely do not. Never have." She rolls off the bed to peruse my DVD collection.

"Well, I might not get it, but if you're happy, I'm happy."

"You know what?" Lilith says, pulling a couple movies off the shelf. "I am happy. I like my life."

"I like your life, too. So, what do *you* want to be when you grow up?"

Lilith puts her hands, holding a DVD each, behind her back and asks, "Left or right?"

"Left."

She doesn't show me the movie but skips over to the player and pops it in.

"I think I'm already what I want to be. I enjoy my job—I love running the front end of the hotel."

"That is so awesome."

"Yeah, I'm pretty cool." She laughs. "What's Benny up to tonight? He didn't want to play with us?"

"He's actually on the annual camping trip with my dad and Danny. It's a thing they've done since Danny was a baby, father-son bonding time, you know. But this year they invited Bennett! He was so nervous, he's never been camping before."

"Aw, that's sweet. Your family really likes him, huh?"

"Yeah, they do."

***

Bennett

"Alright, man, you take the other bedroom. I'll take the couch. Don't want you old men to hurt your backs." Danny laughs, setting his backpack on the floor of the cabin.

"Sorry, Ben," Dan says, rolling his eyes. "I didn't beat that one enough to give him manners."

Chuckling, I reply, "It's quite alright."

I set my bag on the bed in the small cabin bedroom. This place is exactly what you would expect from a log cabin in the forest. Exposed wood, red plaid curtains, peace and quiet.

I had been very anxious about the two-hour car ride with Betty's father and brother. Two hours of conversation, nowhere to escape. But I needn't have worried. Dan is quite content to drive in silence while Danny chatters without expecting a response.

It was nice. Relaxing, even. I felt included but not pressured.

"Come on, let's make a bonfire! I'm dying for a s'more!" Danny says, digging through the bag of groceries.

"Bennett has barely had a chance to sit his bag down, son. Give us old men a damn minute," Dan grumps.

"I'll just get the fire going and you guys can come out whenever, I guess. Won't take me long to get everything going."

He bounds out the door, arms overflowing, letting the screen door slam behind him.

"That boy, I swear," Dan grumbles, settling into one of the recliners that sit on either side of the brown leather couch.

I chuckle. "He's a good man."

"He is, isn't he?" Dan asks. "You know, we've done this every year since Danny was a baby. Never even considered inviting that twerp, not that he would have wanted to come."

"Thank you for inviting me. I've never done anything like this."

"What? Camping? Or this kind of get away?"

"Both," I answer. "My father and I had our own traditions while I was young, but none meant for bonding or relaxing."

Danny stumbles back into the cabin. "Come on, let's cook some shit on sticks!"

"Let's go on out there or he's going to bug the shit out of us." Dan groans, climbing out of the deep seat.

We have barely cleared the door when Danny shoves a hotdog on a stick into my hand.

I brace myself for their laughter. "What exactly do I do?"

"Never had a hotdog before?" Danny asks, barreling up to me.

"I have not."

"Just stick it in the fire until it looks good to you. I like mine burnt."

"We have stuff for sandwiches if you don't want a hotdog, Bennett," Dan says, spearing his own hotdog and thrusting it into the fire.

They aren't laughing at me.

Danny has one in each hand, holding them directly in the fire while slightly rotating them.

"No, thank you. I think I would like to try this."

"You're going to love it!" Danny waves his hotdogs around.

I copy Dan's movements, slowly twisting my wrist to ensure proper cooking.

Danny pulls his out of the fire, they are completely blackened. "I can't believe you've never been camping! Your childhood was fucked, dude."

I bark out a laugh as Dan glares at his son. "Damn it, Daniel Wade. Think before you say shit."

"Sorry, Benny."

"I don't mind. He is absolutely correct. My childhood was... fucked."

"Did your parents do *anything* fun with you?" Dan asks, slathering ketchup on his hotdog.

"Well, I didn't have much of a chance to see my parents as they sent me to boarding school from age five to seventeen," I say, pulling my hotdog out of the fire. It looks very similar to Danny's blackened ones. "However, when I was home my father kept me with him. I would accompany him on his regular schedule. I often attended boardroom meetings, business dinners, and charity galas. I was expected to act like an adult and have conversations about the topics being discussed."

"That doesn't sound fun at all." Danny grimaces.

"How old were you when all that started?" Dan asks.

"I was three, but I learned a lot from it. The social aspects of my life would be significantly more difficult had I not grown up in the business world."

"Yeah, I guess, but—like what about having fun? I know you said you didn't feel like you were missing out but didn't you see other kids playing or something?" Danny thrusts another hotdog in the fire.

"I would compare it to watching a superhero movie. I would see the kids having fun but wouldn't connect it with my life. I was so far removed from other children that it didn't even occur to me to want to play."

"That's wild," Danny says.

I follow Dan's lead and add ketchup and mustard to my hotdog. Tentatively taking a bite, I am pleasantly surprised.

"You like it?" Dan spears another hotdog.

"I do. Very much so."

"Good-o, Benny-o!" Danny shouts, shoving his third hotdog in his mouth.

Dan chuckles, shaking his head.

"Balanced dinner, check! Now it's time for s'mores," Danny declares, rummaging in the grocery bag. Triumphantly he pulls out a bag of marshmallows, a pack of chocolate bars, and a box of graham crackers. He looks at me grinning. "I know you haven't had one of these before!"

I can't help but smile back, his enthusiasm—so much like my Betty's—is infectious.

"I have not."

"They are so good. All you do is shove the marshmallow on a stick, burn it and smoosh it between two crackers with some chocolate. Easy peasy lemon squeezy."

I nod, feeling confident in my ability to burn food in the fire. Too bad Betty doesn't enjoy camping, I think she'd like me making her s'mores.

"So, I uh, I have an announcement," Danny says, looking down, half eaten s'more clutched between his fingers.

"What's going on, son?"

"Well, I wanted to tell you first, Pop, I know Mom is going to freak."

"Should I go inside? To give you privacy?" I ask, uncertain.

"No, no. Stay out here, I'm telling everyone else when we get home. It's not bad! It's good! Really good!"

"Well, spit it out, Daniel Wade." Dan says gruffly.

"So, uh, I'm going to Cambodia. For two years, at least two years."

"What in the hell are you going to do over there?"

"I'm going with this nonprofit, EdWorld, uh, Educate the World. Called EdWorld for short. Basically, places without resources for schools contact them and they send teachers to help the people set up a school. We bring books and supplies, and we train their teachers if they need us to." He shoves the rest of his s'more in his mouth, barely chewing before swallowing. "Usually they don't take fresh graduates, they want folks with experience. But this town needs everything. A school to be built, furnished, and teachers trained. Since I have some construction experience along with my teaching degree, they're going to use me to help build and then assist a more experienced teacher in the training. Probably going to be at least two years—we stay until they tell us that they don't need us anymore. Like, everything is done on the locals' terms. We just bring the experience and resources. It's so cool."

Dan tilts his head to the side. "You sure you're ready for this, Danny? Sounds like a lot of responsibility and you're just twenty-one, barely graduated."

"Dad, I can do it. I want to travel before I settle down and start teaching in San Remo or Verbania, you know? And they need me. They don't have enough volunteers to meet the requests, and I want to help." He slaps his burnt marshmallow in between two crackers.

"If you're sure, I support you. You know your momma is going to cry, right?"

Danny sighs. "I know."

I take my first bite of s'more and it's marvelous. I'll have to acquire a fire pit for our backyard. Betty would enjoy this part of camping. After finishing my treat, I pull out my pocket notebook and make a note to research Educate the World. The Sterling Corporation funds many charitable organizations and this one sounds phenomenal.

I also note that we need a fire pit.

"May I ask you some financial questions?" I look at Danny, who is wiping chocolate from the corners of his mouth.

"Sure," he replies, shrugging.

"Do you have to pay your own way or does EdWorld offer compensation?"

"Well, we don't receive a salary or anything like that, but they do find us lodging, usually with host families in the area. And we get a per diem for food and basics and stuff. Sometimes a company will sponsor an excursion, but donations are low right now. The waiting list is years long, this particular town has been on the list for like five years."

I'm never impulsive but maybe Betty is rubbing off on me.

"I'll sponsor this venture. In its entirety. And I will have my people look into a regular donation to the organization."

"Wait, what?" Danny asks, eyes wide. "You can't be serious!"

"I am serious. Unless I am overstepping?"

Worry washes over me, I don't want to alienate Betty's family.

But then Danny rushes up and hugs me. "Thanks man, this is so awesome!"

Startled, I pat him on the back. "You are very welcome. This is quite the worthwhile endeavor."

"Danny, let the poor man go before he changes his mind." Dan chuckles.

I quickly say, "I would never—"

"I know that," Dan interrupts me with a wave of his hand. "I was just joking. I know you're a man that keeps his word."

"Yeah, I'm literally thrilled that Betty is marrying you. Like, thrilled. Even before you decided to sponsor us," Danny chirps.

My heart pounds, I need to write this down. This... acceptance. *Dan and Danny like me. Actually like me.*

Twenty-Three

Betty

"DARLING, PLEASE KEEP IN mind that my parents are nothing like yours. I do not want your feelings hurt when they are not warm or excited about our engagement."

I smile at him and tug his tie until his lips meet mine.

"As long as you're warm and excited about our engagement, I don't need anyone else to be," I say, watching him relax beneath my words. "Now then, let's go have dinner with the dragons."

His laughter fills the car before he gets out and circles around to my side to help me out. My hand in his—as it has always been—we walk into Rosette, his parents' favorite restaurant in Coslada.

Immediately, I am consumed with insecurities. The women here are sleek and thin, all muted colors—they look expensive. I feel like trash with my bright red hair and black off-shoulder wiggle dress, with my ridiculous cleavage practically bursting out the top. I'm a pigeon with a cinched waist surrounded by swans.

I hold my head high and hope that Bennett isn't embarrassed by me. He looks devastatingly handsome in his deep gray suit and lavender shirt, which brings out his hazel eyes. His gorgeous brown hair is freshly trimmed and styled back off his face. Love for this sweet man swells my heart.

The hostess leads us to an elegant older couple—Bennett's parents. The man looks like an older version of Bennett, down to the gray suit. The woman is beautiful, with perfect blonde hair twisted in a chignon and dripping in pearls.

"Father, Mother." Bennett greets them with a head nod. His father stands up and shakes his hand. "May I present my lovely fiancée, Betty Miller? Betty, these are my parents, Bennett and Tiffany."

His mother gives me a once-over with a pinched smile as his dad shakes my hand.

Once the introductions are done and we sit, the two Bennetts start talking business with numbers and names flying all over the place.

"So, Betty, what do you do for work?" Tiffany asks, barely looking at me.

Shit, shit, shit.

I glance at Bennett, but he's focused on the conversation with his father and doesn't hear his mother's question. We didn't discuss how to frame my career as a smut author.

Well, honesty is the best policy and I suck at lying.

"I write romantic short stories and work in a bookshop."

Please don't ask for details.

"Oh, romantic short stories? How interesting. What publication do you write for?"

"I don't. I self-publish on the Sterling app and a few other sites."

"That's a cute little hobby. And you live on your income from working at the bookstore?"

"Pretty much."

Bennett pats me on the leg, and I meet his eyes, quickly feeling reassured. I shoot him a wink, and he does that little smile that I love so much.

His mother looks between us, her eyes narrowing. "Bennett, are you aware of what your fiancée writes?"

His eyes smolder right there at the table. He looks at me, then calmly replies, "Yes, Mother. I am very aware."

"Well, good. I don't want anything to come out that would embarrass you—or the company."

"Tiffany, I raised Bennett in this company. He would never jeopardize it," Bennett Senior interjects.

"Of course," she says.

**

"Well, that went well," Bennett says, buckling his seatbelt.

"Did it?" I ask skeptically.

"Of course, do you not think so?"

"Well, no. I don't think your parents liked me at all. And I need to learn French!"

His head tilts, bemused. "Darling, I warned you about them. They don't like anyone unless you have something to offer them. I do not believe that they dislike you. But please, do not let them hold any space in that beautiful head of yours. Why do you need to learn French?"

"Your mother looked like she might actually die of humiliation when you explained the menu to me."

"My mother will get over it. I enjoyed showing you the menu," Bennett turns to fully face me. He puts his hands on my cheeks and continues. "Luckily, the next time we have to see them is at the wedding. And we will be much too busy enjoying ourselves for you to worry about them."

I grab his tie to pull his lips to mine.

***

"Your mom just asked if I want to go shopping with her today," I say, as Bennett straightens his tie. I love watching him get ready for the day—seeing him go from rumpled in my bed to a hot CEO is one of my favorite things.

"You do enjoy shopping. I'll leave you my credit card so you can keep up with Mother if you choose to go. Don't feel obligated."

"I can afford my own shopping." I laugh.

"I do not doubt that, darling. But please allow me to spoil you in the same manner that my father spoils my mother."

"Well, if you insist. But just this one time." He raises one eyebrow at me. "Fine, twice. But three times is my limit!" I squeal as he leans over and tickles my ribs before kissing me.

"I must go, though I really do not want to. You look delicious this morning," Bennett growls against my neck.

"I'll still be delicious later," I say, kissing him one last time.

The front door alarm chirps as he engages it. So I roll over and open his bedside drawer. Pulling out his navy blue notebook, I snag a pink glitter gel pen and write a silly little love note for Bennett to find later.

I hate when you leave for work in the mornings but I love watching your ass as you walk out the door. Also, I adore you.

***

"You simply must try this on." Tiffany hands me another sad beige dress. I look at it and die a little on the inside. Every time I find something I actually like, she has something negative to say.

I really do need some more... wealthy-looking clothing, I suppose. For Bennett's business things and all that. I guess I can't always wear tight clothes with bright colors.

She hands another beige something to the sales associate to take to the fitting area. I'm glad that Bennett gave me his credit card. I actually cannot afford to keep up with his mom. Somehow I already have more clothes than my savings account can afford being delivered to our home—and it isn't even lunchtime yet. Tiffany assured me that this is what is expected of a Sterling wife. I can return them if Bennett is upset. He assured me that I can get anything my heart desires, but this is so much.

And my heart doesn't desire any of it.

"There. Once we finish here, we can have lunch. Then we will go to the salon," Tiffany says, gesturing to the sales girl.

"Oh good, I'm starving! I forgot to eat breakfast this morning."

"Yes, well... maybe you should do that more often," she replies, looking me up and down. Again.

I tug up my top, totally self-conscious. Every single thing I've put on, she has a comment—if I had shapewear it would lay better or how it just isn't made for people with my shape. I've always loved my body, but now I'm worried that Bennett might be embarrassed to have me on his arm. When his mother saw me this morning wearing black pedal pushers and a cute black halter top with pink polka dots, she asked if I was wearing a costume.

"Ma'am, I have your fitting room ready. Follow me, please," the perky, slim associate says.

The fitting room is a nightmare—a mirrored octagon that forces me to see that silk makes me look lumpy from every angle, and that neutrals aren't my color.

"That looks decent enough. We have to get you good shapewear—though that won't help nearly as much as I'd like. And we really have to do something with your hair. It clashes terribly with everything."

"I don't want to change my hair," I protest.

"Nonsense, this looks like you did it at home. I think a nice chocolate brown would suit your complexion nicely. We do want you looking your best for Bennett, don't we?" she asks with a dismissive wave of her hand.

I thought my hair looked nice. Bennett always compliments me, but maybe he's being kind. I mean, what is he supposed to say? That I look like cheap trash? He would never.

"I guess so," I reply, trying not to cry. I excuse myself to the restroom, my heart pounding, and call Bennett.

"Hello, dearest. Is everything alright?"

I'm thrown off by his hurried tone. "Uh, yes. I just... hi. I wanted to say hi."

"Hello, my love. Can I call you back in a couple hours? I would love to talk but unless it's urgent I have a meeting to get to."

"I'm sorry! I'll let you go!"

"I love you, darling. I will call you back as soon as I get a few spare moments," he says.

"Don't worry about it, I just wanted to hear your voice. I love you."

I take a few deep breaths and blink quickly, trying to force the tears back. A few fall anyway. Damn it. I fix my makeup and exit the restroom to find Bennett's mother waiting for me.

"Let's go have lunch. A nice salad will sustain us for the rest of our day."

"I think I'll just go on home afterwards." I'm so ready for this whole thing to end.

"Nonsense. We have an appointment at the salon. Then we'll pop into Elamour."

"I definitely don't need to go by Elamour. I have more make-up than I know what to do with."

"Yes, well. None of it is appropriate, I'm sure. Especially once we fix your hair," Tiffany says with a grimace.

"I don't think I should change my hair."

"I'm sure Bennett has filled your head with compliments—as he should. However, a powerful man like my son expects a certain type of woman. One that his business associates won't leer at and hit on. Let me help you so that you do not embarrass yourself. I'm worried about you."

A heavy weight settles on my shoulders as I follow her out of the store. I'm crushed—and just plain sad. I've been too busy having fun with Bennett to really consider what life with a super-successful CEO would actually be.

I don't have time to think before I find myself in a salon chair, with my future mother-in-law directing the stylist. Bennett calls, but she answers for me.

I need to talk to Bennett.

I'm foggy, panicky, and so uncomfortable. I need to scream but can't form a sound.

Now my hair is brown, and I'm in a makeup store. My lipstick is garish, my eyeliner too dark. Why would I ever wear baby pink blush? Thank goodness his mother is here to help.

Time is passing in a blur. I'm so disconnected from everything.

Then I'm home and nothing's right. But Bennett will be here in about an hour, so I really should shower and get ready to show him the new me.

***

Bennett

I'm excited to see Betty's new stuff. She didn't want me to spoil her, but I love it. She deserves every single thing that she wants, and I aim to make sure she has it. I should have demanded more of those high heels, though—maybe some bright blue ones. They would look so good on my shoulders.

I hope Mother didn't talk her into cutting her hair. Not that she wouldn't look enchanting with shorter hair, but it's the perfect length to get my hands in.

I do love her so.

"Honey, I'm home!" I yell, walking into the house. Expecting my Betty to come bouncing down the stairs, I smile up at the top of them.

I am not prepared for the beautiful, elegant woman who appears at the top of the stairs. Her hair falls in a shiny brunette waterfall around her shoulders. A tan dress lightly skims her body, hiding her curves.

She looks amazing—but not like *my* Betty.

She walks to me slowly, a small smile on her face. Out of all of the outcomes for today this is one I never imagined.

My Betty is vivacious and bright. This Betty is neither.

I don't like it.

I want my vibrant red-headed Betty, not this muted socialite. I open my mouth to tell her that, but stop myself when she looks up at me with hopeful eyes.

I don't want to hurt her feelings.

"You look amazing, darling. Absolutely beautiful."

Her smile trembles—did I say something wrong? But then it brightens. I must have been mistaken.

"Thank you!"

I pull her into my arms and kiss her. She doesn't kiss me back with the enthusiasm that I have come to expect from my Betty. I touch her face—and my phone rings, jolting us from the moment.

"I'm sorry, dearest. It's work. Would you like me to silence it?"

"No, no. Of course not. Take your call," she says sweetly.

I sigh and answer, not liking what I hear.

I rake a hand through my hair. "I'm sorry, my love. I have to go back to the office. That kid Lukas has some accusations against Bill—including embezzling, among other things. I really need to see to this."

Shock flashes over her lovely face. "Poor Lukas! He's not in trouble, is he?"

"I don't think so, dearest, but I won't know until I look through the files."

"Okay, I'll probably have dinner at my parents' house since it's been a couple weeks."

"Oh, good. I hate to leave you alone," I reply, pulling her to me and pressing a kiss on her now chocolate hair. "You really are so beautiful. I can't wait to peel this off of you later."

She giggles but it doesn't feel right. I will have to talk with her later tonight to check in. I glance at my watch, knowing that I need to rush. It'll take me at least an hour to get back to the office.

"I just might let you," she says as we walk to the door.

***

Betty

"What the fuck happened to you, Pigeon?" Danny asks, horror evident on his face.

I texted him to meet me at our parents' house—we arrived at the same time.

"You don't like it?" I run my fingers through my new dark hair.

"Fuck no. I hate it. You don't look like Betty."

His words settle around me, as does the realization that *this* is the reaction I wanted from Bennett. I don't want his mother to be right. I want Bennett to love me for me—bright red hair, tight clothes, and all.

My eyes fill with tears—so many tears. The stress of the day, Bennett's reaction—it all crushes me.

I miss my red hair. I hate my new clothes. These shoes pinch my toes.

Before I know it, I'm bundled up in my parents' home, on their sofa, with my whole family looking like murder is on the horizon.

"Bethany Rose, you need to tell us what happened before your dad and brother run off acting crazy in the wrong direction," my mom says, knowing full well she is the most likely to act crazy. She's never played about her kids.

"Bennett's mother thinks I'm trash, and dyed my hair, and I bought so many ugly dresses. And I think Bennett likes me like this," I sob.

"That bitch! I want to talk to her right up close," my mom snarls, making me laugh through my sobs.

"She's right, though. You should have seen me at that fancy restaurant. I stood out so much, and then I couldn't read the menu because it was French. She hated me from the very beginning." I sniffle and hiccup.

"What did Bennett say about that?" Danny asks.

I lift my shoulders. "He and his dad were talking—I don't think he realized. Then today he had a work thing and I barely even saw him. But he said I looked so good like this. I don't want to change but what if he wants me to?"

"I think you're jumping to conclusions," my dad says.

"You sure he wasn't telling you what he thought you wanted to hear?" my mom asks gently.

Looking down, I say, "I doubt it."

"But you don't know for sure! Bennett isn't close to his parents. How would she know what he likes?" Danny asks.

"She said that I would embarrass their family. I don't want Bennett embarrassed." I cry.

"Bennett is a good boy. I think you need to talk to him, Betty Bunches." Mom rubs my hands between hers.

"I'll talk to him if you want me to." Danny stands up.

"Daniel, sit down, son. Betty is a grown woman. She's gotta handle this herself," Dad tells Danny before turning to me. "Now, Betty. Bennett has shown himself to be a good man and nothing like that twerp you were married to. Talk to him. You solve nothing by running away."

I roll my watery eyes and slump back on the floral sofa. "I know. I just needed to talk it out a little bit."

"Now, let's go have some cake and cry a little." Mom drags me into the kitchen.

***

Bennett

"We appreciate you bringing Bill's misdeeds to our attention," I say, shaking Lukas's hand.

"Thank you, sir."

A bright chime rises up from my pocket, alerting me to a message from Betty.

Could you meet me at my parents' house when you finish at work?

I reply in the affirmative, my heart pounding. This situation is out of the ordinary. I never go to her parents' house to see her after work. Unless it's movie night—but it's too late to start a movie tonight.

***

Betty's parents' house is the kind of house you imagine when told to think of a house. Three bedrooms, red bricks, and a wooden front door. A white porch swing and hydrangeas complete the look.

I knock on the door—surprised when Danny answers solemnly.

"Hiya, Benny. She's in the kitchen," he says without his usual exuberance, then walks off.

I'm hit with an overwhelming urge to run away. To leave as fast as I can. To escape. And if it were anyone but Betty, I would.

Instead of running, I step inside, nodding to her dad in his recliner as I pass by. Betty and her mother sit at the kitchen table, a cheesecake between them. Betty doesn't giggle and run to me. That hits like an arrow to the heart. Her mother raises an eyebrow as she stands and walks out of the room.

I want to apologize, to beg Betty not to leave me, to demand that she stay and marry me. I need to find out what is the matter, then I can fix it.

I hope I can fix it.

I sit in the chair that her mother vacated and really look at my Betty. The straight chocolate-brown hair, the barely-there make-up. Her tear-stained cheeks. Her bloodshot eyes.

I'm crushed under her despair, under this feeling of wrong.

I can't stand this distance. I reach out and drag her into my lap, grateful that she doesn't resist.

Instead, she cries.

I can't speak. I can't do anything but hold her. I rub my hand along her back, grateful that she allows me to do this.

"Darling, please tell me what is wrong so I can fix it," I beg.

She sobs harder.

My panic is palpable. I can taste it.

I reach for a paper towel and gently blot her tears. She smiles, bringing my panic down to a manageable level, and takes the napkin from me.

Sniffling, Betty pulls back, her eyes puffy, and asks, "Do I embarrass you?"

Shock ripples through me.

"What? Of course, you do not embarrass me. Please, dearest, tell me what you're thinking."

"Your mother said I embarrass you. She thinks I look like trash. And I'm not even sure how I ended up getting my hair dyed. I hate it so much. But you loved it, so I thought... I thought you would rather I look like this," she wails.

Anger like I've never known shoots through me.

How dare that woman make Betty feel like anything less than an absolute goddess?

"That is absolutely not true. I love you—and I love everything about the way you look. I prefer your red hair and fun outfits over this muted version of you. I had no idea that my mother would act like this, and I am so sorry. You will never have to see her again," I say, squeezing her and peppering kisses all over her face.

"I can't do that to you. What about holidays and such?"

"Dearest, my parents are not like yours. What you saw at dinner is what all of my interactions with my parents are like. Mostly business-related and always impersonal. I spend the holidays alone. It is no hardship to cut my mother from my life. I will continue my meetings with my father, unless you'd rather I see neither of them?" I ask, studying her beautiful, puffy face.

"No, of course not. And you can't do that to your mother—not over me. I'm too sensitive. She probably didn't mean any of it the way I took it."

"I can do anything I want, and I will when it comes to your happiness. You are the most important thing in my life, and I will not have anyone disrespect you. Especially not my mother. And you are not too sensitive. You are the perfect amount of everything—there is not one thing that I would change," I reply, running my fingers through her silky hair. "Well, except your hair and clothes. I would like those to go back to normal."

Twenty-Four

Bennett

"WHAT THE FUCK DID you do to your hair?" Stella asks, stomping into the kitchen with her lip curled in disgust.

I tense, ready to tell Stella off for talking to Betty that way, but Betty laughs and says, "Bennett's mom got a hold of me."

Stella whips her glare to me.

"You left her alone with your mother? That was stupid."

Guilt washes over me. "Yes, I see that now. At the time it seemed a marvelous chance to spoil my fiancée."

Betty, as usual, knows what I need and tosses herself into my lap.

"Leave him alone, Stells. He feels bad enough already." She wraps her arms around my neck.

"He should! Look at you! Are you going to fix your hair?"

"I want to, but I don't really know where to start." Betty huffs. "I've always done my own hair but I don't know how to remove color without making my hair fall out. And I'm kind of nervous to go to a salon—what if they make it worse? I just want to go back to my red hair and not deal with this," Betty whines, making my heart lurch. I am not a fan of displeased Betty. She should always be happy.

"We'll have my daughter come over tomorrow," Stella says. "She's a hairstylist and loves doing fun colors. Bennett'll pay her well and she won't fuck you over."

"Oh, I don't know... I wouldn't want to put her out or anything like that," Betty says, uncertain.

"Tell your daughter that I will pay her triple what she makes in a day to come here and make my Betty comfortable again," I tell Stella, squeezing Betty tighter against me.

"Well, there you go. Jada will definitely not be put out to hang out with us and earn three days of pay." Stella smirks and starts tapping away on her phone.

Betty kisses me on the cheek and lays her head on my shoulder.

"Thank you, Bennett."

I try to hold on to my guilt, knowing that I deserve it—but Betty is curled up in my arms, making it impossible to feel anything but content.

***

Betty

"You're going to have to learn to stand up for yourself, girl," Stella says, exhaling a plume of cigarette smoke.

We're sitting on the cute front porch swing that Bennett installed for me. I loved my little loft on the other side of town, but this house that Bennett found for us overlooking the beach is truly my dream come true. Salt air whips our hair around as the swing squeaks beneath our weight.

I sigh. "Yeah, I know. I just... things don't hit me right away. I freeze up in the moment, get overwhelmed, and can't think. Then hours—or even days—later I realize what happened. But it's too late then."

"Well, that's a fucking problem, isn't it?"

"Sure is."

Heavy metal fills the air as a beat-up red Camaro pulls into the driveway.

"There she is and only fifteen minutes late." Stella chuckles, taking another drag.

"Shut up!" yells the leather-clad Jada. I can see her resemblance to Stella, but Jada has her head shaved and a face full of jewelry.

Jada drops her cigarette on the ground, stomps it out, and then picks it up, asking, "Where do I toss this?"

"Right over here, doll," Stella says, gesturing to the snazzy cigarette trashcan that Bennett has out just for her.

"Cool."

Jada finally looks at me—up and down—and grins. "You are stunning. We are going to have so much fun today. You definitely should *not* be this boring-looking. I mean, what were you thinking, dying your hair mud brown?"

I didn't really get dressed today. I'm wearing Bennett's old hoodie, which shows off his prestigious attendance at Folkstone University, and a pair of black yoga shorts. My newly brown hair is pulled up into a messy bun. I haven't even brushed it—it makes me cry to look at it.

Stella snaps, "Filter your fucking thoughts, Jada. Her bitch of a mother-in-law pulled a fast one and here we are."

"Want me to send her a gift certificate to my salon and accidentally shave her head?" Jada asks, using air quotes around accidentally.

Laughing, Stella says, "She wouldn't be caught dead in the area that your salon is in. But damn, that would be so fucking funny."

Once the giggles die, I sigh and say, "No, she really didn't do anything wrong. I let her railroad me in her effort to turn me into someone that Bennett could be proud of."

Stella's smile snaps into a glare. "Shut your mouth with that bullshit. Bennett is, and always has been, proud of you. She is a closed-minded hag—and you'd do well to remember that."

"Hell yeah. Now let's get you sorted out," Jada says.

We set up a salon, using the kitchen table as the beauty station. It's almost like being kids again, with Jada mixing potions and painting my hair. I don't ask questions—I let her work, listening to her and Stella chatter around me.

"Alright, hot stuff, we've got all of the shit-brown out of your hair. Now we get to decide what color we're going to do on you." Jada digs through her box of goodies.

"Red!" Stella and I say at the same time, laughing.

"Well, okay, then. No pink or blue? Nothing shocking?"

"Nope. I just miss my red hair."

We chat a bit more about tone and scroll through pictures on Jada's phone before settling on the perfect cherry red.

***

Bennett

This has been the longest day that I can recall. Knowing that my Betty is at home repairing the damage that my mother caused, it's torture.

With that thought in my mind, I dial my mother's number.

"Hello, Bennett. To what do I owe this unexpected call?" My mother's crisp voice answers.

"I am going to keep this short. You will not be invited to the wedding and I would appreciate if you have no further contact with my fiancée."

"May I ask why?" she snaps.

"You were unkind to Betty. Simple as that. I will have no one, especially not you or father, disrespect her."

"She is wholly unsuitable to be your wife."

"Goodbye, mother."

I hang up the phone for once feeling sad about my family situation. My cold upbringing never bothered me before falling into

Betty's family. Their warmth and easy acceptance feel like magic. It's no wonder that Betty turned out as wonderful as she is.

Betty will let me know when her hair is done and she is ready for me to come home. However, I am unable to concentrate on work until then. I decide to see if Danny wants to meet me for lunch—he never minds when I talk about Betty.

We agree to meet halfway between our jobs, at a little sandwich shop.

"Hey, Pigeon's Benny, how you doing?" Danny asks in his usual exuberant fashion. I didn't expect to become close to Betty's brother—he is significantly younger than I am—but I find his similarities to Betty to be refreshing and I genuinely enjoy spending time with him and the rest of my Betty's family.

"Pigeon's Benny? I think I like that. I've never asked—why does your family call her Pigeon?"

"She hasn't told you?" Danny laughs. "It's hilarious. So I'm like nine years younger than Betty, so I don't really remember her being chubby, but then she, I don't know, got her figure. But I remember my mom bought her some new clothes—this was when she was just getting into this whole look she has going. And my mom said 'You look like a pigeon with a cinched waist.' We all cracked up. Especially Betty. She started cooing at us and for the longest time she would point at one of the birds and say 'There's my real brother,' and shit like that. It became our favorite family joke. And pigeons are Betty's favorite bird, so it just works."

I pull out my pocket notebook to write down this story for my *Betty Book*, but Danny snatches it from my hand.

"Please don't open that," I say, reaching for it.

He hands it back to me with a chuckle. "I'd never do that. What do you keep writing in there?"

"I don't recall personal facts easily. So I note anything mentioned in conversation that I might need to remember later. When I know that I will see someone, I refresh my memory."

"That's freaking brilliant! I should start doing that—but I'd probably lose the notebook. Just end up with like twelve half-used ones scattered around."

Warmth surrounds my heart at Danny's praise. I'm not used to people encouraging me unless it's about business. As if I might have worth outside of my ability to earn money.

It's a revolutionary concept that Betty and her family have thrust into my life.

"Yes. It wouldn't work well if you lose them."

"So what's Pigeon up to today? Doesn't she usually have lunch with you if you're not busy?"

"She is spending time with my housekeeper and her daughter, repairing the damage to her hair," I say, sullenly.

"Oh, thank god. All that shit your mom did to her was horrible."

I exhale slowly, guilt creeping up my spine. "Yeah, I've told my mother that she is not invited to the wedding and that she is to never contact Betty again. We will never have a repeat of that day."

"Damn, dude. You cut your own mom out? Over Betty? That's fucking awesome. She deserves that—for once."

"I aim to give Betty everything that she deserves."

"I can see that. That's why we all like you. We thought she was going to waste her life on that twerp, then—there you were."

"Yes, with a mother who made her question her worth."

"But you stood up for her. The twerp always took his mom's side. A horrible mother-in-law is not new for her. She doesn't need you to protect her but just back her up."

"I fully plan to do both," I say firmly.

***

Betty

"Wait, girl. Let me grab you one of your outfits while Jada does your makeup. That way you can see the whole you—put back together again." Stella stops me as I hop up to run to a mirror.

Jada finished my hair and I'm anxious to feel like me again. But Stella's idea sounds even more fun. I haven't had girlfriends in a really long time—Trevor managed to chase them all off by our second year of marriage. Guilting me into canceling plans, cutting phone calls short... Eventually, they all fluttered away.

"Yes! Like playing dress up with a grown doll! Let me grab my kit!" Jada says, dancing out the front door.

Stella laughs, pats my shoulder, and stomps toward my room. "Hot pink or blue today?"

"Pink!"

Jada dances back into the house, startling Yogurt with her big rolling makeup case bumping behind her. The little cat hisses and runs out of the room, her collar jingling as she goes.

"Alright, Ma said that you do rockabilly retro, yeah?" Jada asks, popping open the case.

"Yeah. I stick with a red or pink lip and winged eyeliner."

"I can see that. Alright, let's make your man drool when he sees you," Jada replies, quickly picking out products.

My excitement jolts up at the thought of Bennett seeing me. Knowing that this is how he prefers me—it's just... perfect.

***

Bennett

Stella's name pops up on my caller ID, raising my anxiety. "What's wrong?"

"Nothing's wrong. You left her with me. Now, I was just calling to let you know you're free to come home. Jada is fixing to do Betty's makeup, and then she'll be all back to normal again. You can stop your worrying."

"Thank you, Stella. I will be home as fast as I can."

Stella hangs up without saying goodbye—a trait that I appreciate. No fake pleasantries are needed with her.

It only takes me a few minutes to leave the office. I barely register Jake, my new receptionist, calling goodbye as I rush into the elevator.

The drive home is endless. Traffic crawls. It feels like I will never see Betty again.

Pulling into our driveway, I spot Jada and Stella leaning against a red Camaro, smoking and laughing.

I sit for a second trying to calm my racing heart, then step out of the car.

I nod at them as I rush toward the house, their laughter following me.

The front door opens as I reach the bottom step.

I'm frozen in place at the sight before me.

Betty—my Betty—has to be the most wonderful thing to ever exist. I cannot imagine a sight that I would prefer over her, in the doorway to our home, wearing a tight pink halter dress. Her bright red hair is styled in curls and her lips the perfect shade of pink.

I'm lovestruck.

Immobilized, all I can do is stare.

I watch her blush and nervously smooth her hands down her dress. That whisper of insecurity breaks me from my trance.

"Betty, my love, you are magnificent," I say, my throat tight. I rush up the stairs and sweep her into my arms, my mouth crashing onto hers.

Stella and Jada cheer in the background, but I can't focus on anything that isn't Betty.

She giggles against my mouth, and I crowd her until she steps back into the house. My hands roam her body—I can not get enough.

***

"Father. To what do I owe this call?"

"Bennett. You cannot exclude your mother from your wedding. It's unseemly."

"I can and I have. The way she treated my fiancée was unseemly, and I will not have a repeat."

"She was merely doing what is necessary. Your fiancée is wildly inappropriate for a man of your stature. Now, what you *will* do is apologize to your mother and have her take over the wedding planning. I cannot imagine what tacky affair your fiancée would arrange. Nothing appropriate for a Sterling, that's for sure."

Fury floods my bloodstream as I snap, "Neither you nor Mother will be at my wedding. This conversation is over."

"You will do as I say. I'm sure your fiancée is a good time but she is wholly inappropriate—"

Blinded by rage, I slam my fist into the table.

"This conversation is fucking over. Never contact me again," I roar into the phone, slamming it down.

A timid knock snaps me out of my rage spiral.

"Sir, is everything okay?" Jake asks from the other side of the door.

Needing to get out of the office, I fling open the door, startling Jake, who holds a nervous hand over his heart.

"Cancel all of my meetings. I am going to be unavailable for the rest of the day," I say, walking right by him.

"Yes, sir," he calls out timidly to my retreating back.

I need to see Betty. To make sure she is okay. That she still loves me.

The drive home is brutal, traffic and the distance gnawing at me. When our perfect pink house finally comes into view, I rush through the front door—greeted by Yogurt and her tinkling bell.

"Bennett?" Betty calls from the top of the stairs. "Is everything okay?"

I rush up to her, pulling her into my arms and walking her backward until she's pressed against the wall. I need to feel her warmth. Knowing what I need—what I can not express verbally in this moment—Betty wraps her arms around me and lets me hold her, my face buried in the crook of her neck.

I wish I had a better family to offer her. A family like hers that cares more about *us* than appearances.

Betty squeezes me and rubs my back. "Why don't we go lay down?"

"Could we do it naked?"

"Of course."

***

I awaken with a jolt, naked, with my head on Betty's bare breast. I take the opportunity to suck her delectable nipple into my mouth, making her breathe in sharply and tighten her arms around me.

"Bennett!" She gasps, playfully surprised.

I release my treat and look up at her. She's smiling, but her eyes are clouded with concern.

"Ready to talk about it?" She asks, running her hands gently up and down my back.

"I love you, so much."

This brightens her smile, and she replies, "I love you, too."

I sit up, needing to look her fully in the face. Her luscious breasts distract me momentarily—they are large, heavy, and amazing. I want them in my mouth. Instead, I tug the blanket up to cover them. She giggles, knowing I can't talk with her openly naked.

"I'm sorry that I can not offer you a kind family to marry into," I say.

Her eyes fill with tears.

"I'm sorry that you didn't *have* a kinder family to grow up in."

"That is of no importance. But I want you surrounded by love, and my family can not even offer basic decency."

"I *am* surrounded by love. I don't need anything from your family, except you. I just wish that they were better... for *your* sake. Not mine." She puts her hands on my cheeks and guides me into a gentle kiss.

"I spoke with my father today," I say once I pull back.

Betty doesn't say anything and reaches for my hand. The way she always knows what I need and offers it so freely heals every wound left on my soul by my parents.

"I've cut both him and my mother out of our lives."

"I hate that," she says sadly. "I never wanted to cause problems in your family."

"You haven't caused one single problem. Your light has only illuminated the problems that were already there. I hold no affection for my parents, and I am sure they feel the same. We were merely obligated to each other, and I severed that bond. No one treats you with anything but the utmost of respect." I fling the blanket off her and pull her soft body into my lap. "Besides, you are my family. My parents caused problems with my family. Not the other way around."

Betty's head on my chest, my arms around her, I let myself ponder the strong reaction I had to cutting my father off. Outrage over his treatment of Betty, yes, but there's more to it. Something deep-seated, a sadness that I never let myself experience. Now that I've become close to Betty's family, it is glaringly obvious how much I missed in my childhood. Betty's family is full of inside jokes and affection. I would bet my entire net worth that my parents couldn't tell me one story from my youth, let alone one that means something.

My heart aches, but my arms are full of my future. A future full of affection and laughter.

A future that I'll build with Betty.

Twenty-Five

Bennett

"ALRIGHT, Y'ALL HAVE A good ten-month anniversary meeting. I'm hitting the road," Stella says, wiping her hands on the towel draped over her shoulder.

"It's our ten-month *relationship* meeting. Gah, get it right!" Betty laughs, walking Stella to the door.

I set out our china and light the candles, carefully arranging them on the table. The front door clicks shut, and Betty's arms are around me, her face pressed into my back. I rub her hand as I finish setting the table.

"It's beautiful, Benny-Boo," Betty says, unraveling her arms from around me.

I take her hand and help her into her seat, her pretty face glowing in the candlelight. I'm mesmerized. When she flushes and giggles I realize that I have been standing here and staring at her a little too long.

"Forgive my staring, darling. I seem to be unable to keep my eyes off of you tonight." I move into my seat.

Preening, she retorts, "Maybe later you won't be able to keep your hands off me."

A laugh breaks free. "My dear, I always struggle with keeping my hands off of you. All I want to do is touch you."

"And yet, here you are, so far away." She pouts, looking at the half-foot of space between our chairs. Since the very first night I met Betty, we have sat on the same side of the table—right next to each other. The few times we've been forced to sit across from one another, I have felt the loss acutely. I crave the warmth of Betty's body next to mine at all times.

I slide my chair away from the table and pull Betty into my lap, nuzzling her neck. She sighs and relaxes into me.

"We aren't going to get anywhere in this meeting if you keep that up."

I sigh, knowing it's true, and allow Betty to clamber back into her seat.

"Yes, well. Meeting first, and then you are all mine to touch."

We settle in comfortably and try the incredible meal that Stella has prepared for us. She always goes all out for our relationship meetings, knowing how important they are to Betty and me. Tonight's feast is reminiscent of traditional Thanksgiving fare—turkey with all of the side dishes. She always makes way more than we can eat, the Sunday leftovers are delightful.

Betty is effervescent as she chatters on about her latest book and the happenings at the bookshop. When her stories come to an end, I steer the conversation to our wedding.

"Shall we discuss wedding details?" I ask, and watch her joyful expression cloud over.

"Yes, uh, what kind of wedding do you want?" she replies, with little enthusiasm.

This change in demeanor is so unlike Betty that I'm momentarily stunned into silence. A strange feeling of terror overrides my system.

Does Betty not want to marry me?

The urge to run and write these feelings in my notebook overwhelms me. The only thing keeping me grounded is Betty herself, picking at her food, discontent dripping off of her.

Once again, I slide my chair away from the table—but this time I also take Betty's chair to turn her to face me. My heart breaks seeing her sad eyes. This simply will not do.

"Darling? Tell me what is the matter so I can fix it," I beg, dread creeping in as Betty's eyes fill with tears.

"It's stupid," she says.

"Nothing you say in this moment could ever be stupid. Please allow me to make this better for you."

"I just, I know you have to have a fancy wedding. CEO Bennett Sterling and his gajillion dollar wedding, right? Invite all of your business people and impress them and all that. I'm just disappointed. Maybe I kind of did want an Elvis impersonator or something. But the wedding really doesn't matter, because you will be my husband!" She pats me on the leg.

For a moment, I can't speak. It stuns me to think she's been carrying this, quietly convincing herself she doesn't get what she wants. That I might love her, but not listen to her. That is the deepest horror of all.

I cannot bear this distance and tug her into my lap, this time straddling me.

"My dearest love, the only thing I have to do is make you happy. I don't care about the size of our wedding or who is invited, as long as it pleases you."

"But your mother said—"

I cut her off with a quick kiss and say, "I do not care what my mother said. You matter. We matter. I will always be sorry that I allowed my mother anywhere near you."

She sniffles, a tear trailing down her face. "That wasn't your fault. You thought it was just a shopping trip."

"Regardless, your happiness is my responsibility—and I failed."

"You didn't fail," she says. "You've always made me happy. So what if your parents suck? That isn't your fault. If you don't need a huge fancy wedding, then what kind of wedding are you thinking?"

"Good change of subject, my dear." I study her face.

"Thank you." She sniffles.

I grab a napkin and pat her tears away—trying not to wipe her makeup off. She giggles and snags my tie to pull me to her. Forgetting everything, my lips meet hers and the world is perfect.

Too soon, my future wife pulls away and smiles at me. Like sunshine peeking out from behind a grey cloud.

"Now, let's plan your dream wedding."

"*Our* dream wedding," she retorts, her tone dripping with sass.

I tickle her side, enchanted by her laughter. "Calling you Mrs. Sterling—that is my dream. The party is quite irrelevant to me. So please, tell me what you want, and if anything sounds unpleasant to me, I will tell you."

"I want it small and fun. And I'm serious about that Elvis impersonator."

"Then that is what we will have. Allow me to get us a new notebook for our wedding. I believe I have a white one in the closet."

Betty claps her hands and kisses my cheek before climbing off my lap. "White is perfect for a wedding notebook!"

Before Betty crashed into my world, I had no need of so many journals. One for my pocket and two at my bedside. But this vibrant woman has brought so much life with her that it can't be contained in only three notebooks. A smile erupts onto my face as I look at the stack of empty journals I have at the ready. Before, my notebooks were somber colors—but now it's a rainbow in my closet. I grab a white one and hurry back to my Betty, looking ethereal in the candlelight.

She wiggles in her seat as I get settled with a pen.

"Small, fun, and an Elvis impersonator." I write them down.

"Yes. Now what do you want?" she asks, grinning at me.

I look at her for a long second, thinking about my answer. I write down one word before turning the page for her to see.

Betty.

Tears fill her eyes as she finds her way back into my lap. She snags the pen and puts a single check beside her name on the list.

Squeezing me tight, she mumbles into my chest, "You really don't care?"

"I only care that you love it. Just give me a list of what you want, and I will make it happen."

"I love you," Betty says, her voice muffled.

I kiss the top of her head. "I love you, too, dearest."

***

Betty

"Come on in. I gotta get my shoes on then we can go. Now, what are we doing? I heard you but... didn't." Lilith laughs, sliding her feet into purple sneakers. She's dressed for a full day of shopping, wearing a short, flowy, buttery yellow dress and her hair in purple Bantu knots.

"We're shopping for my honeymoon trousseau."

"A troo-what? Explain this to me like I'm five, please." Lilith bounces all over the room, turning off twinkle lights and her sound machine. The sudden loss of birds chirping feels stark in such a soft environment.

I chuckle. "Come on, let's hit the road," I jingle my keys. We walk out, Lilith locking the door behind us.

"So, a trousseau is basically a new-wife lingerie assortment. It was started ages ago to give chicks linens and pots and pans and stuff, but now it's mostly just for naughty things. I think most girls just have a lingerie shower, but you're the only person I would invite to one of those—so we might as well do it together."

"Fucking nice! Remind me of this if I ever find a man," Lilith jokes, climbing into the front seat.

Bennett gave me a credit card with my name on it and told me to use it for anything wedding related. I haven't touched it yet—haven't decided on anything for our wedding.

Except lingerie. I've never really worn anything other than cutely practical underwear and Bennett is already obsessed—he is going to lose his mind seeing me in something lacy and sheer.

We're going to start this marriage off with a bang.

"I definitely will! I'm pretty excited about it. I want a full collection—from sensual to downright lascivious, you know?"

"Yes! I'm an underwear girlie, so this is my happy place of shopping. Where are we going?"

I start the car and navigate out of the parking garage, waiting until I'm on the road to answer.

"Xavira," I say, waiting for her reaction.

"Oh. My. God. Seriously? *The* Xavira? Like, no shit?"

"Yup. And I'm going to get you some things too, as a thank you."

"No! I can't let you! Getting to look around will be enough for me," Lilith says breathlessly.

"You can let me, or else I won't get anything either. We'll just cancel the appointment and go to the mall."

"No! No. Maybe I can let you buy me just one little thing. Oh my god. I'm going to own a brand new Xavira!" Lilith exclaims, bouncing in her seat.

Okay, I get it now. I see exactly why Bennett likes to dazzle me with expensive gifts. This reaction? It makes my heart happy.

The hour-long drive goes by fast, the air full of merriment and sparkles.

Lilith gets quiet when we pull into the parking lot of the snazzy underwear shop.

She takes a deep breath, looks at me and says, "Thank you." She waves her hand around. "Not for the nighties, or whatever—but for this. I don't make friends easily. I'm usually home alone. This is really nice of you."

"Oh shush," I lightly slap her arm. "Before you, my only friends were my mom and brother. I feel like *you* are doing *me* a favor."

"Damn it." She shakily exhales, blinking rapidly and looking up. "Alright, no crying while shopping. We're friends. You like me and I like you. Okay."

I laugh. "Exactly! Now let's go buy things that will make my fiancée's head explode!"

As we walk arm and arm into one of the most exclusive lingerie shops in the world, I'm hit with emotion.

This is my life. A best friend and a man that thinks the sun shines out of my ass. A year ago, this was only a dream.

***

"No, you *totally* have to get this one! It's crotchless! You need less crotches in your tro-whatever!"

"Don't you think it's too much? I already have, like, twenty sets! Oh my goodness, I'm going to max out this credit card!" I say, a whisper of panic infiltrating my dreamy day.

But Lilith chortles and waves a dismissive hand. "He's a bujillionaire, I doubt you could max this card out if you bought a house and a car too."

"I just, I don't want to seem like I'm after him for his money or anything."

Lilith rolls her eyes and hangs the black negligee back on the rack. "Yeah, buying lingerie with *Bennett* in mind, for your *honeymoon*, is totally going to raise some red flags."

"Shut up. Fine. Give me the crotchless one."

"Here—and this one too. Maybe get that other one in a couple colors, it looked really good on you." Lilith hands me another handful of spicy outfits to add to my ever-growing pile.

The salesladies hate us. We walked into the store laughing and shattered the elegantly silent vibe they had going on. Once again, I felt like a pigeon surrounded by swans—but this time I had Lilith. She winked at me and asked for a couple fitting rooms.

When they told us that they only accepted appointments, I knew it was my time to shine. Well, my fiancé's time to shine, technically. I gave them Bennett's name and watched their attitude change before our eyes.

That was *super* cool.

They tried to tuck us into a fitting room and bring selections, but after the fiasco with Bennett's mom, gorgeous blondes picking out my clothes is a hard no.

So here we are, champagne in hand, giggling over some of the most expensive lingerie in the world.

Twenty-Six

Betty

SEARCHING THROUGH WEDDING WEBSITES and how-to articles, one thought rises to the surface—

I don't want a wedding.

I don't know what to do. My wedding dress is finished and oh, is it gorgeous—below the knees, A-line with a sparkly lace overlay on the bust. It gives me cleavage galore, and Bennett is going to lose his mind. The veil is so cute—very Audrey Hepburn with a little bow.

But.

I'm miserable. I simply do not care what the tables look like, or what food everyone will eat. Bennett and I agreed on 25 guests, but even that seems huge. I want something silly, fun, private. Only Bennett and me—like our engagement. I want to focus on Bennett, not all of these other people. I don't want to listen to little speeches from people who aren't in our relationship. I want to hear Bennett tell me that he'll love me forever. Privately.

I want our day to be about us and only us.

I'm overwhelmed—hands shaking, heart pounding, can't catch my breath.

I don't want a wedding.

I need to talk to Bennett. I hope he isn't disappointed. If he is... maybe we could hire a wedding planner. Yes, that's what we should do. I won't even mention not wanting a wedding. I'll tell him that I don't want to plan one.

And maybe Bennett and I can exchange private vows afterwards.

He's working from home today. I should poke my head in and talk to him really quick.

Anxiously, I tap on his office door. Seconds later, a chair squeaks, footsteps approach, and the door opens to Bennett smiling at me—a smile that is quickly shadowed by whatever he sees on my face.

"Betty, darling, what's wrong?" He takes my hands and pulls me into his office.

"I don't want a wedding!" I blurt out, horrified. Bennett's eyes widen in shock—and hurt—and I hate that I put it there.

"You don't want to get married?" he asks, tugging me into his lap, his hands shaking and voice tinged with sadness.

I smoosh my face into his neck, breathing in his woodsy scent, and mumble, "I don't know what I want."

He tightens his arm around me, his fingers stroking gently through my hair.

"What are you thinking? How can I help?" His voice is rushed, almost panicked. I pull back to look at him—devastated by what I see. His precious face is pale, eyes shining with tears.

His question finally clicks in my brain.

You don't want to get married?

"Wait—no. I do want to get married. To you. I want to marry *you*. But just us two, you know? I don't want to invite anyone. I'm overwhelmed. I don't want a wedding. I'm sorry."

His whole body tenses and relaxes as he takes a deep breath and shakily releases it.

"So we're alright?" he asks, uncertain.

I tug his tie until our lips meet—softly, so softly.

"We're perfect," I whisper against his mouth.

Another shaky exhale, his forehead against mine.

"Would you like to fly to Vega Luz and have Elvis marry us?"

"Really? You won't be mad at me?"

"Of course not. I'm happy when you're happy," Bennett says, kissing my head.

"Can we go tonight? Just go and get married?"

"I, uh—yes, well. Could we wait until this weekend?" He stammers, reluctance in his voice.

I pull back to look at him, his face is bright red.

"This weekend will be perfect! Why?"

"Well, I had a suit custom made—and with the right amount of incentive, I'm sure they can have it completed by this weekend. Plus, I would like to hire a photographer. If that is okay with you?" He asks, his tone unsure.

"Very okay, but can we keep this a secret until we get back? I really want it to be just us. I don't even want my parents wishing us luck or anything. What kind of suit?"

He chuckles, clearly relieved and says, "Patience, my dear. The suit is a surprise. And yes, we will keep all of this between us until you are ready to let the world in."

***

Betty

The house that Bennett rented is absolutely stunning. The backyard is a perfect desert oasis, with fountains and cacti—I love it so much that Bennett offered to buy the whole place for me.

Bennett is determined to document every moment of our wedding, including a first look before we run down the Vega strip looking for a chapel. The photographer, Annie, is outside with Bennett, snapping photos of him in his custom suit.

A suit I haven't seen yet.

I'm so excited that I can barely keep myself from looking out the windows—I don't want to ruin Bennett's surprise.

I'm trying to keep my dress cat-hair free but it's a struggle with Yogurt weaving herself through my legs. I itch to pick her up and get some kitty cuddles but settle for a scratch under her cute little chin.

"Betty?" Annie calls into the open window. "It's time for the first look. Go out the front door and to your left. Follow that sidewalk into the backyard and stop at the gazebo."

I race down the path, vibrating with energy, and find the pavilion. I bounce on the balls of my feet, waiting anxiously for Bennett. Annie comes from around a corner, telling me to stand just so and reach around the ivy-covered wall. I find Bennett's warm hand and grasp it, wanting to pull him around. Annie snaps the pictures, adjusting our positions before each one.

"Alright, now step around the wall, Betty, and let's get those first looks!" Annie chirps.

Oh, Bennett is so handsome.

His suit is surprising, dove gray with an almost unnoticeable light blue checked pattern. Not what I was expecting at all. He's never worn a patterned suit before.

His eyes fill with tears. "Oh, darling, you are stunning," he says reverently, like he can't believe I'm his.

I fling myself into his arms, unable to get close enough to him.

"We're getting married!" I gasp.

"That we are, my dear," he whispers, squeezing me even tighter.

"I love your suit," I tell him, leaning back to see his precious face.

His smile brightens as he says, "I had it custom made with your love notes."

He instructs me to look closer at the blue thread—it's made of words!

My words!

The check pattern is actually my little love notes embroidered.

"I put your first note on the chest pocket," he says, pointing to my stitched words *Betty loves Bennett.*

I lean into Bennett, knees weak. I can't speak. Can't think.

He loves me so much.

His strong arms tighten around me, supporting me when I cannot stand on my own. And isn't that just like Bennett?

"Ready to get married, my dearest love?" He whispers, our foreheads together.

***

Standing outside *Hunk O' Burning Love Chapel,* I whisper, "I think this is the one."

Bennett grins down at me. "I think so, too."

We've been popping into wedding chapels along the Vega strip, searching for Elvis—and the right energy. This one is cute, looks like a little white country church, but has a neon sign above it touting the name and a pair of hearts with cupid's arrow through them. Most importantly, there's a sign in the window proclaiming *Elvis is in the building.*

I squeal and pat Bennett on the arm, shimmying my shoulders with excitement.

The inside matches the outside, cute and quaint with the right amount of Vega edge.

Elvis greets us with a booming "Hey there, baby!" and just like that, I know—we picked the perfect place. I give Bennett a quick nod. He grins down at me before turning to introduce us to *the* Elvis. We pick our wedding package and start filling out the paperwork, hands trembling.

We're ushered into the chapel, a riot of kitsch and color. The walls are covered with artificial flowers, while neon signs buzz with declarations of love and burning desire. Red vinyl pews line a hot pink aisle that leads straight to the altar—a plush red velvet heart crowned with gleaming gold flames. On either side, toddler-sized white Cadillacs sit among a flock of pink flamingos, our perfect wedding guests.

Can't Stop Loving You plays softly as we walk down the aisle toward Elvis.

It's perfect.

***

Bennett

A year and a half ago, I couldn't imagine a life outside of business. My days were drab and predictable—until Betty. Betty, who pulled me out of an awkward situation and shined a light into every corner of my world. And today, like a dream come true—a dream that I never dared to dream—I get to marry the most magnificent woman on earth.

My Betty is ethereal. The glow from the windows illuminates her like a goddess. Soft lace covers her shoulders but frames her cleavage like a priceless work of art. Her baby blue heels match the embroidery on my suit perfectly—like I knew it would.

I can't stop looking at her. Can't stop touching her. Can't stop making sure she's real.

Betty looks up at me, eyes shining, her hand in mine as she repeats those magical words, "I do."

A tear rolls down my cheek as I say the same.

"I do."

"Alright, folks, the moment we've all been waitin' for! You may now kiss the bride, baby! Go on and give her a real good one!" Elvis says, cutting through my thoughts.

Betty laughs as I chase her lips, claiming them as my own.

Twenty-Seven

Betty

MY SUNROOM IS MAGNIFICENT during a rare rainstorm. Rain pelts the glass ceiling in a steady rhythm—soothing, hypnotic. I close my laptop. Tomorrow will be soon enough to finish writing that scene. I turn on some sad girl music and just... exist. I'm not sad. No—I'm quite the opposite. But sometimes, you need to listen to sad music and watch the rain.

Yogurt jumps onto the bed, allowing me to scratch her head before she makes herself comfortable on the pillow near my feet.

The ocean is beautiful—gray clouds over shimmery blue water made rocky by the cloudburst.

"Mrs. Sterling?"

Bennett stands in the doorway. He considers the sunroom to be my space—like his office belongs to him—and always asks before entering.

"Yes, husband?" I answer, loving the small smile that title always brings.

"Would you like to dance in the rain with me?"

Breathless, I nod. My heart pounds as I take his offered hand and follow him onto the balcony. He twirls me around and pulls me in tightly, swaying to the echoes of the music from inside.

I can't be anything but happy.

Within seconds, we're drenched—water running down our faces and into our smiling mouths. My hair falls into my face, plastered over my eyes, and Bennett gently clears my vision.

"Thank you," I whisper, not wanting to break this magical spell.

He lowers his head, brushing our lips together before taking control of the kiss. It's wet and full of fire.

He slowly pulls away before spinning me out and twirling me under his arm. I squeal and laugh, and when I'm back in his arms—where I belong—I grab his tie and pull his lips to mine again.

His hands slide down my hips, pulling me flush against him.

***

"Happy one-year relationship meeting, my love. I do have a serious topic for discussion this time," Bennett says, sitting next to me on the sofa.

Dinner was sublime—Stella really outdid herself—and Bennett had the table covered in lilacs and peonies. He never lets me help out for our relationship meetings. Insists that he wants to do this for me.

"You aren't asking for an open marriage, are you?" I joke, laughing at Bennett's surprised face.

"Of course not!"

"I know you wouldn't do that to me," I say, patting his hand. He flips it over and threads our fingers together before kissing the back of my hand.

My heart skips a beat. "I love you."

"You are my entire world," Bennett replies.

I let go of his hand to straddle his lap, my dress allowing my naked pussy to rub against his crotch. He groans and lifts my skirt to take a peek before quickly pushing it back down.

"You'll be the death of me," he breathes into my ear as I feel him hardening beneath me. He runs his hands under my skirt to grab my ass cheeks roughly, grinding me down on his hard cock.

I smile and whisper in his ear, "What did you want to talk about?"

He moans. "My penis in your pussy—that's what I want to talk about."

I giggle. "That sounds serious, Mr. Sterling."

"Oh, it is, Mrs. Sterling, very serious. It requires your immediate attention."

"Oh, does it now?" I murmur, lips curled in a teasing smirk. I swirl my hips, rubbing against his length.

His head drops to the back of the sofa as he groans, his hands sliding down my thighs. I lean forward and kiss him, soft and slow, then stand up. Languidly, I unbutton my shirtdress, never taking my eyes off of his flushed face.

Sliding the dress off my shoulders, I'm left standing in a pink, sheer lace bra—and a smile.

"Darling, you are exquisite. Can I touch you?"

"You can always touch me." I unsnap my bra, letting it fall to the floor.

And then I'm in his arms, his mouth on mine, and I'm pulling his shirt off. He lifts me up and I wrap my legs around him as he carries me over to the couch and tosses me on it. I bounce with a giggle but then Bennett is grabbing my thighs and pulling me to the edge of the sofa. Burying his face between my legs, he sucks my clit into this mouth, leaving me half dizzy and needing more.

The mouth on this man.

"Bennett, please, more..." I whimper.

He lifts his face, my juices glistening on his chin. His finger finds my button, moving in slow circles, building heat in my core.

"Tell me what you want," he demands.

"I want your cock."

"Give me an orgasm first." He dives back in, groaning like I'm the best thing that's ever been on his tongue.

He sucks harshly on my nub, shoving two fingers inside me, and my orgasm crashes over me. My legs—tossed over his shoulders—tense around his head. He gentles his tongue as my trembles slow, licking and nibbling softly.

"Flip over, darling. Hands on the back of the sofa."

I assume the position, arching my back so he gets a full view of my pussy and ass. He groans and rubs his hands over my cheeks before squeezing. I feel his thick cock at my entrance—he slowly, so slowly, pushes in. Taking his time, he fucks me leisurely, running his hands over every inch of skin that he can reach—finally landing on my breasts. He finds my nipples, stroking his thumbs over their hardened tips.

It's too much and not enough. So perfect, but more.

I need more.

"Bennett..." I whine.

"Tell me. Whatever you want. It's yours—demand it, my love." He rasps, breathing heavy against my neck.

"Harder. Fuck me harder!"

Bennett breaks open, all restraint gone. Skin slapping against skin, teeth on my back. His hands pull on my nipples, sending lightning through my veins. I reach between my legs, rubbing in time with his thrusts.

I cry out as I shatter, completely undone. Bennett follows me into bliss, shouting my name.

Foggy with pleasure, Bennett arranges us on the sofa. We lie tangled together, my heart still racing, my mind finally still. The room smells like us—warm, spent, at peace.

My head on his chest, I slowly regain my senses.

"Alright, babycakes, now that we've cleared our minds..." I giggle into his chest. "What was it that you wanted to talk about?"

He tightens his arms around me and kisses my forehead. "Well, I think we should discuss children."

"Children in general or a specific child?"

His chest rumbles under my cheek with laughter. "Our future children, actually."

"Oh," I say, sitting up on the couch.

His eyes slip from my face to my tits, then back up to my face.

"Oh?" he asks.

"Yeah, I don't know how I feel about having kids. I thought that I definitely wanted them before, you know. It was what you do, right? Get married and have babies. But with you, I'm really enjoying it being just us two. Do you want kids?"

He pulls himself into a sitting position. "At this time, I don't have strong feelings either way. I love spending time with you alone. And I am not a huge fan of change, so I would be quite fine with not having children in the foreseeable future."

"Okay, that's good. I think I want children—but not any time soon, you know?"

"Well, then we should shelve this discussion for a few years. Maybe in five years, we can revisit the idea?"

"Yes, let's do that!"

Bennett takes my hand gently, and brings it to his lips. "I love you, darling."

***

Bennett

Our love is like cotton candy—fluffy, soft, and so sweet I could cry.

Mouth dry and heart pounding, I take the love note and place it back in my notebook for safekeeping. My desire for Betty cancels any other thoughts—I need to see her.

Soft music floats down the stairs, so I follow it to find Betty lying on her daybed in the sunroom, clad in my old Folkstone sweatshirt and thigh-high socks. Hopefully, that's all she's wearing. The desire to touch her skin is overwhelming, so I gently knock on the door frame, never barreling into her space.

She rolls over and smiles at me, eyes wet with tears, mascara tracing rivulets down her cheeks.

I rush in, scooping her into my arms. "My love, are you alright?"

She laughs, sniffles, and reaches for her discarded book. "This thing is so freaking sad!"

"I'm sorry that it's doing that to you."

"I'm not! I needed a good cry," she says, wiping the mascara with the sleeve of my sweatshirt.

Unsure of how to respond to that—or why one would need to cry—I hug her more tightly to me and kiss her forehead.

She giggles, cuddling closer. "It's like, crying is a release, right? And I'm so happy that I don't get to cry, really cry, very often. So reading sad books lets me cry and still have you."

I fall in love with her all over again. Every single day.

***

Betty

"Look! Let's get cotton candy!"

"Why would I need cotton candy when I have you, darling?" Bennett replies, kissing the side of my head and maneuvering us through the crowd toward the cotton candy booth.

"Maybe I need sweetening up?" I laugh.

"You have always been the sweetest thing in my life. But if my wife wants spun sugar, my wife gets spun sugar."

We join the long line for the sweet treat and watch the rest of the carnival-goers ramble around us. Everything has a golden hue in the setting sun and the day has been perfect. I've pushed Bennett onto multiple rides, and he won me a lime-green unicorn that I immediately gave to a crying little girl. The area smells like beer and funnel cake. I love it.

I spot someone with a hot pink drink and pat Bennett on the arm. "Ooh, Benny-Boo, I need one of those too! Doesn't it look fun?"

He laughs. "It does, my dear. Would you like me to go find one for you while you wait for the cotton candy, or shall we stick together?"

"Do you mind? That would be perfect. We're supposed to meet up with Lilith soon."

"I'll keep a look out for her."

He kisses my nose, then the back of my hand, and heads out to find the drink of my dreams.

"Bennett!" I yell, waiting until he turns back. "Get Lils one too!"

"Of course."

I turn back to the cotton candy machine, where gossamer sugar swirls and a woman expertly winds the fluff around sticks before shoving it into bags.

"Betty!" Lilith calls from somewhere in the crowd. I look around, trying to find her—there she is! Wiggling through the sea of people, she finally makes it to me.

"I found Bennett, and he told me where you were. Figures you'd be getting cotton candy." Lilith chuckles, sliding next to me in line.

"Hey! I haven't had any all day!" I reply, digging in my purse for my wallet.

I buy four bags of cotton candy so Lilith and I can enjoy a couple of bags now, and then I get some tomorrow, too!

"Bennett should buy you a cotton candy machine!" Lilith says, jamming a piece of sweet fluff into her mouth.

"Then you'd never leave!"

"Boo!"

"How was work?" I ask her, finding a spot on the grass to sit and watch the fireworks. They should begin right at nightfall, so we don't have that much time to wait.

"Bennett!" Lilith yells, startling me. I turn and look behind us, finding Bennett walking our way, two snazzy pink drinks in hand.

Lilith and I accept the drinks, adjusting ourselves on the grass so Bennett can join our little group.

"Long time, no see!" Lilith says to Bennett, elbowing him in the side.

"Yes, ten minutes is an eternity," he jokes.

I lean my head on his shoulder. He wraps an arm around me, tugging me closer.

Flashes of the past explode like the fireworks we're watching.

Trevor. Betrayal. Solo dates. And Bennett. Always Bennett. No matter the path I took, I was always meant to be right here.

Five Years Later

Betty

"You are the most beautiful baby in the world, yes, you are," I coo, looking into little Poppy's sweet blue eyes.

The couch shifts as Bennett sits next to me, his large hand gently cupping baby Poppy's head. I look into his hazel eyes and fall even more in love with him—he is so gentle.

"I think it is my turn for a cuddle," he says, taking the baby from my arms.

I kiss his cheek. "Alright, I'll go make a bottle. She'll be hungry soon."

He smiles up at me before looking down into the baby's face. The love radiating from him takes my breath away.

Humming to myself, I start making a bottle. I can't help but sneak another glance at Bennett and Poppy—she looks like she's smiling at him.

And then she farts. Loudly.

I laugh, and Bennett looks horrified.

"Darling, I think she defecated," he says, gagging slightly.

"What do you want me to do about it?" I ask, slowly backing away.

The front door flings open, and my brother stomps in. "Where's my baby girl?"

"Oh, thank goodness! Your daddy is here to change your stinky butt," I say, taking Poppy from Bennett's arms. I kiss her and hand her off to Danny, who grumbles about aunts and uncles that never change diapers as he starts to undress her.

"Well, darling, I do believe that our job here is done," Bennett takes my hand. "Danny, your daughter is delightful until she starts to smell."

"Ain't that the truth." Danny laughs.

In the car, Bennett threads our fingers together and raises my hand to his lips. "My dear, would you like to open the discussion on having children? You are quite enamored with little Poppy."

"Oh, shush. You were just as enamored as I was."

"This is very true. She is a lovely baby," he says, smiling.

"She is. But I still think I like it just the two of us. How about you? Do you want a baby?"

"I do not. I would prefer to visit with your brother's baby and not deal with the messy parts."

"I agree."

10 years later

Betty

TODAY'S THE DAY.

Situated between Enchanted Verbania and Verbania Sweets and Treats is my baby: *Lovestruck Verbania*. Fable wanted to focus more on children's books and general fiction, simply not having the space for a full romance section. So I did it. I worked overtime on my smut empire—as Danny calls it—and saved every single dollar to be able to do this: open my very own romance bookstore.

Bennett offered to buy it for me years ago, but I needed to do this on my own. And I did.

I freaking did it!

Looking in the mirror, I add one last bobby pin to my cute victory roll and hope it stays rolled when I let go.

It doesn't. *Figures.*

Muttering expletives under my breath, I quickly brush out my hair and call it good enough.

"Darling, are you ready?" Bennett inquires from the doorway, looking as handsome as ever in his gray suit and pink tie. I smooth down my hot pink A-line dress and double-check that the halter is lying flat against my neck.

Turning to him, I ask, "How do I look? Like a business owner?"

He smiles at me, grabs my hand, and pulls me to him. "You look amazing, my dear."

The nerves really hit as we walk onto the porch of our pink house, and I stop, tugging Bennett back.

"I can't do this."

He takes my face in his hands and says, "You already have. All you need to do today is smile and cut that pink ribbon. You've done all the work these last few years—now it's time to accept your congratulations. Lilith said that a line has already formed at the door of *Lovestruck*. You have to go let them in."

"What if they hate it?"

"They won't. It's amazing."

"Are you sure?" I ask, tugging his tie until his lips meet mine.

"Positive. This is your moment—enjoy it. Let's go have fun."

Too anxious to walk, Bennett drives me to the center of town. I'm vibrating with excitement, unable to sit still.

Maybe we should have walked.

When my building comes into view, the anxiety vanishes like it was never there. It's perfect. A sweet baby blue with pink accents and so cozy on the inside that you can't help but lounge in one of the overstuffed chairs with a nice cup of tea and read.

I can't believe it. A crowd really has formed around my store. And up front—my family. They're all standing beneath the sign that says *Lovestruck Verbania*, waiting to welcome me home.

I take a deep breath. With my hand in Bennett's, we walk into my bookshop—ready for our next adventure.

About the Author

Lovey LaRue creates stories about emotionally intelligent men who are ready for love and women who never have to change to be worthy of it. Her characters live authentically and find love in the little moments. At home, she juggles a couple of teenagers and a husband who've made peace with sharing space with her imaginary friends. Between family life and pets—a Siamese cat named Ginger and a Basset Hound mix named Rocko—she hasn't had a minute alone in twenty years. When she's not slowly losing her sanity, she's usually hiking or building book nooks.

www.ingramcontent.com/pod-product-compliance
Lightning Source LLC
Chambersburg PA
CBHW021409110726
47901CB00008B/2121